Enid Blyton™

KITTY at St CLARE'S

Written by
Pamela Cox

D1438078

EGMONT

EGMONT
We bring stories to life

First published in Great Britain 2008
This edition published in 2010
by Egmont UK Limited
239 Kensington High Street
London W8 6SA

Text copyright © 2008 Enid Blyton Ltd, a Chorion company
Cover illustration copyright © 2008 David Roberts

The Enid Blyton signature is a registered trademark of Enid Blyton Ltd,
a Chorion Group company.

The moral rights of the cover illustrator have been asserted

ISBN 978 1 4052 3038 4

A CIP catalogue record for this title is available from the British Library

Typeset by Avon DataSet Ltd, Bidford on Avon, Warwickshire
Printed and bound in Great Britain by the CPI Group

Contents

Where's Pat?

Isabel O'Sullivan and her cousin Alison sat in the small station café drinking cups of tea and eating jammy buns. Both girls were waiting for the train that would take them back to St Clare's after the holidays.

'Mummy dropped us off here far too early,' complained Isabel, who was bored with the wait and Alison's company, and longing to see some of the other third formers.

'That was my fault,' said Alison sheepishly. 'I thought that the clock in your kitchen was slow. Sorry.'

Isabel swallowed the last of her tea then, glancing out of the window, brightened as she saw a group of girls in the familiar St Clare's uniform walk by. But they turned out to be top formers and sailed past without so much as a glance at the two younger girls, which made them feel very small indeed. Isabel sighed. 'I shall miss Pat terribly,' she said for about the fiftieth time.

'Well, you have plenty of other friends in the third form, and Pat will be back in a couple of weeks,' pointed out Alison with commendable and – for her – unusual common sense.

Isabel nodded, though she still felt miserable. She did have lots of friends at St Clare's – good friends. But it just wasn't the same as having her twin with her. Alison just didn't understand what it was like to share everything, even thoughts and feelings – to be so close to someone that they were almost a part of you. How she had hated leaving Pat this morning. And how Pat had hated being left behind!

'You will write, won't you?' her twin had said anxiously that morning. 'Every week. And tell me all the news.'

'Of course. But what a pity you won't be able to write back.' Isabel had tapped the plaster cast on Pat's right arm.

'Don't worry about that, Isabel,' Mr O'Sullivan had said. 'Pat can dictate her letters to me and I'll write them out for her. I shall be her secretary!'

That had made both girls laugh, but when the time came for them to part they had felt more like crying.

'Now we must be sensible about this,' Pat had said briskly, seeing Isabel's chin begin to tremble. 'We shall be together again very soon, after all. Besides, if we start crying that will set Alison off. You know how she loves a good blub!'

Alison had taken the teasing in good part, laughing and punching her cousin playfully on her good arm, so the twins had parted on this lighter note. But, for Isabel, some of the pleasure she always felt in going back to St Clare's was gone.

'I say, Isabel!' cried Alison suddenly. 'Isn't that Bobby and Janet over there?'

'Yes – and Hilary too!' said Isabel, forgetting her woes for a moment and jumping to her feet so hastily that she almost upset the table. 'Come on, Alison, let's go.'

The two girls dashed out on to the platform, calling out, 'Hi, Bobby, Janet! Hilary, wait for us!'

The little group of third formers turned round, their faces breaking into delighted smiles as they saw their friends.

'Hallo, Isabel. Hallo, Alison. Nice to see you again!'

'Had good hols?'

'Isn't it grand to be going back to school! I say, where's Pat?'

'She's broken her arm,' explained Isabel dismally. 'It's her right one, so Mummy decided there wasn't much point in her coming back to school until it's healed.'

'Golly, what rotten luck!' exclaimed Hilary. 'How on earth did she manage that?'

Isabel grinned. 'She took it into her head to pay a visit to the old tree-house that Daddy made for us when we were little. I warned her that the branch wouldn't bear her weight and I was right.'

'Ouch!' said Bobby. 'Poor Pat.'

'Most undignified behaviour for a third former,' said Janet, pretending to be shocked. 'Seriously, though, I'm terribly sorry. How long until she comes back?'

'Two or three weeks, the doctor thinks,' answered Isabel. 'So you others will have to put up with me

3

hanging around you until then.'

'Well, I daresay we can put up with you if it's only for a short while,' said Bobby with her wicked grin. 'Oh look, here comes Jenny.'

The third formers turned to see Jennifer Mills of the sixth coming towards them, a pleasant smile on her kindly face.

'Hallo, you lot,' she greeted them cheerily. 'I expect you've all heard that I'm to be head girl this term as well as games captain. So if you have any worries or problems I'm always on hand to help.'

'Thanks, Jenny,' said the third formers rather shyly. They all looked up to her enormously. Yet, as Hilary said, when the older girl had moved away, 'There's something so lovely and warm about Jenny, even though she's so sensible and dignified. You really feel as if you could tell her your problems and she would listen and take an interest.'

The others agreed, then Janet said, 'Now there's someone I wouldn't like to share my troubles with – Margaret Winters.'

The others looked round as another sixth former approached. Margaret was a remarkably good-looking girl, with straight dark hair cut in a dramatic bob, unusual violet-coloured eyes and high cheekbones that gave her a rather exotic appearance. She also looked extremely haughty and it seemed as though she would pass by the third formers without a word. Then her glance fell on Alison and she saw the way the girl was staring up at her, eyes wide with admiration. Margaret liked admiration. She bestowed a dazzling smile on the girl, said 'Hallo, Alison' and favoured the others with a brief nod before passing on.

'My word, Alison, you're honoured!' exclaimed Hilary. 'Fancy Margaret, of all people, speaking to a mere third former.'

Alison said nothing, staring raptly at Margaret's retreating figure.

Bobby nudged Isabel and said slyly, 'Looks as if your cousin has found someone else to worship. Alison, don't say you're going to lose your silly heart to Margaret Winters.'

Alison's habit of idolising the most unsuitable people was a standing joke among the third formers and the girl turned red, saying defensively, 'Nothing of the sort. Though I admire her tremendously, of course. She's so attractive and has such poise and self confidence!'

'Yes, it's just a pity her character doesn't match up to her looks,' said Janet dryly.

'That's a terrible thing to say!' cried Alison. 'I'm sure I don't know what you've all got against her.'

'She's sly,' said Hilary. 'And spiteful. Last term she made one of the first formers learn a great long speech of Shakespeare's and recite it to her, simply for cheeking her a little bit.'

'Quite right too!' said Alison indignantly. 'Some of those kids are far too full of themselves and they need to learn a little respect for the top formers.'

'Don't waste your time,' murmured Isabel, as Hilary opened her mouth to say something else. 'You know what Alison's like once she's decided that someone's worthy of her adoration. The more you try to put her off Margaret, the more she will stick up for her!'

'I suppose you're right,' said Hilary with a rueful grin. 'I say, isn't that our train along there? May as well find ourselves good seats before the crush starts. Come along everyone!'

The girls hurried along the platform, then Janet suddenly tapped Bobby's shoulder and said, 'I wonder what's going on over there? Looks like some kind of row.'

The third formers turned their heads and saw two new girls standing facing one another. Both had their hands on their hips and, judging from the angry scowls on their faces, were exchanging heated words, while their embarrassed parents tried to calm them down.

'Friendly looking pair,' said Bobby wryly. 'I suppose they must be sisters, although they don't look much alike.'

Indeed they didn't. One girl was fair and slightly plump, while the other was dark and slim.

Suddenly Miss Jenks, the second-form mistress, bustled across and said something to the girls' parents. The sisters themselves immediately fell silent, quite awed by her authoritative tone and air of dignity.

'Helen, you come with me and I'll introduce you to some of the second form,' said Miss Jenks to the fair girl. Then she glanced across and spotted Janet, beckoning her over. 'Janet, this is Amanda Wilkes, who is to be in your form this term,' she said, placing a hand on the dark girl's shoulder. 'Take her under your wing for a bit, would you?'

'Of course, Miss Jenks,' answered Janet proudly. She was to be head of the form this term, and making the new girls feel welcome was one of her duties. She waited patiently while the two girls said goodbye to their parents, then Miss Jenks led Helen away and Janet took Amanda's arm in a friendly way, saying, 'It looks as if the others have boarded the train. Let's join them and I'll introduce you to everyone.'

The third formers looked up with interest when Janet came into their carriage with the new girl. She looked a little nervous, and no wonder, thought Isabel, giving her a friendly smile. It must be quite an ordeal starting at a new school where the others had all known one another for ages.

'Everyone, this is Amanda Wilkes,' said Janet. 'Amanda, meet Isabel, Alison, Hilary and Bobby.'

'Nice to meet you, Amanda,' said Hilary. 'Is this your first time at boarding school?'

'Yes, and I've been looking forward to coming to St Clare's so much,' replied the girl. 'I just wish Helen didn't have to tag along and spoil everything for me.'

The girls were rather shocked at this. What a terrible thing to say about one's own sister. Isabel couldn't imagine ever feeling like that about Pat and said, 'I should have thought it would help you settle in, having your sister with you.'

'Helen isn't my sister!' said Amanda, obviously horrified at the very thought. 'We aren't related at all really.'

'Oh,' said Bobby. 'When we saw you both together with the two grown-ups, we just assumed that you must be sisters.'

'She's my *step*sister,' explained Amanda. 'You see, my father died when I was a baby, and Helen was only little when her mother died –'

'Then your mother met Helen's father and the two of them hit it off,' said Janet.

'That's right,' said Amanda gloomily. 'They married a few months ago.'

'Well, you don't sound awfully thrilled about it!' said Alison. 'Don't you get on with your stepfather?'

'Oh yes, he's a dear,' said Amanda. 'And Helen absolutely adores Mummy. It's just one another that we can't bear!' Suddenly the girl became silent and looked around, giving a self-conscious little laugh and turning red. 'Heavens, just listen to me! I've only known you for five minutes and here I am telling you my life story. You must think I'm simply dreadful!'

'Ah well, we're such kindly souls that few people can resist confiding in us,' said Bobby, making everyone laugh.

'And it's certainly broken the ice,' said Janet. 'You're one of us now, so you can tell us anything you please and know that we won't pass it on.'

'Gosh, thanks awfully!' exclaimed Amanda, turning pink with pleasure at being so readily accepted by these jolly, friendly girls. 'I must say, it is good to get it all off my chest. You see, my stepfather is very wealthy and he's spoilt Helen all her life, letting her have everything she wants. She's the most frightful little snob as well.'

'I shouldn't worry about that,' chuckled Isabel. 'She'll soon have her corners knocked off at St Clare's.'

'Yes, the second formers will sit on her all right,' said Hilary. 'You just wait, Amanda! In a few weeks' time she'll be a much nicer person.'

2

An unusual schoolmate

The train girls switched to a coach once they arrived at the little station near St Clare's, and after a short journey their beloved school was in sight.

'Look, Amanda,' said Janet. 'If you look to the left you can just see St Clare's in the distance – that big white building.'

'Yes, I see!' cried Amanda excitedly. 'My word, it looks simply enormous.'

'That's what Pat and I thought when we first arrived,' said Isabel. 'But once you know your way around it doesn't seem quite so huge.'

Amanda's stepsister was sitting a couple of rows in front and, overhearing this, said to the second former beside her, 'Poor Amanda! She simply can't get used to living anywhere too big. Of course, she and her mother lived in the *tiniest* little cottage before they moved in with Daddy and me. I remember it took her simply ages to find her way around our house.'

Amanda turned red with fury, her brown eyes glittering as she opened her mouth to make an angry retort.

'Steady,' said Janet, laying a hand on her arm. 'If Helen knows that she's annoying you it will only make her worse. Leave it to her own form to put her in her place.'

Janet was right, for the next moment Grace, the second form's sensible head girl, said coolly, 'Come off your high horse, Helen. None of us are impressed by your big house or your father's wealth.'

Helen looked put out, but one look at Grace's stern little face was enough to warn her against saying any more.

'I told you,' said Janet. 'Just ignore her and she'll soon get bored with baiting you like this.'

Amanda nodded. How much easier it was to deal with Helen when she had people like Janet and Isabel to back her up and offer sound advice.

At last the coach turned into the long drive that led up to St Clare's, the girls' noses pressed up against the windows as they looked out. Isabel frowned. Normally on the first day of term there were girls wandering around simply everywhere. But today there was something different. A huge crowd was gathered on the lawn and there seemed to be some sort of commotion.

'I say, whatever is going on over there?' said Hilary.

'Let's find out,' replied Bobby, standing up and grabbing her night-case from the luggage rack.

The others followed suit and, as soon as the coach stopped, everyone scrambled out and ran to join the crowd gathered on the big lawn. In the middle of it stood Mam'zelle, the French mistress, wagging her hands towards the sky as she always did when agitated. And opposite her stood a small girl with a cap of shiny red curls, a smattering of freckles and the merriest, naughtiest blue eyes the girls had ever seen. But it wasn't she who was the cause of the commotion. In her hand she held a lead and, at first, the third formers thought she had brought a dog to school with her. Then they edged to the front of the crowd and saw that the animal on the end of the lead wasn't a dog, but a small black-and-white goat.

Suddenly Janet spotted their fellow third formers, Carlotta Brown and Doris Elward, who had arrived by car some time earlier, and moved towards them. 'Carlotta! Doris!' she cried. 'What's going on and who on earth is that?'

'Begorrah, 'tis our new girl, Kitty Flaherty,' said Doris, in a fine imitation of an Irish accent, her humorous eyes twinkling. 'She's an absolute scream!'

Then Mam'zelle spoke, her voice shrill as she said, 'This is a school for young ladies, not a farm! And a farm is where this horrid, fierce animal belongs!'

'Bless you, Mam, McGinty is the gentlest creature you could wish to meet,' said Kitty Flaherty, in an accent exactly like the one Doris had adopted. 'Sure and he'll be no trouble. No trouble at all, Mam.'

Mam'zelle stared perplexedly at the girl before her. Why did she speak in this strange manner? And why did she keep calling her Mam?

Just then Jennifer Mills and her friend Barbara Thompson came over, along with Margaret Winters. Jenny and Barbara seemed much amused by the situation, but Margaret was most disapproving. She walked right up to Kitty and, pointing at the goat with an expression of disgust, said, 'What is that?' Margaret was as cool and authoritative as any mistress, even Mam'zelle falling into subdued silence at her presence.

Kitty, however, did not seem at all worried. 'Why, 'tis a goat,' she replied, looking at Margaret in surprise. 'Did you not know? It's a few nature study lessons you need, I'm thinking.'

The listening girls roared with laughter, Janet clutching at Doris and gasping, 'Oh, she's simply priceless!'

Everyone waited for Margaret, not noted for her sweet temper, to explode, but she contented herself with a sharp, 'Don't be cheeky! I can see that it's a goat. What I want to know is, what is it doing on school premises?'

'Ah, yes!' put in Mam'zelle, recovering herself. 'That is what I, too, wish to know. A school is no place for goats! The good Miss Theobald will be most upset and angry when she hears of this.'

'But Miss Theobald knows all about McGinty,' said Kitty. 'Sure and I have her written permission to keep him at St Clare's, Mam.'

'And do not call me Mam!' cried Mamzelle, feeling that she was losing control of the situation. 'I am Mam'zelle, do you hear?'

At this point Miss Theobald herself, having been alerted by someone, arrived on the scene. The first day of term was always an extremely busy one for her, and she looked annoyed at being interrupted. 'What on earth is going on here?' she demanded. 'Goodness gracious, a goat! Would someone care to give me an explanation?'

Mam'zelle and Kitty both obliged at once, the Frenchwoman's exclamations of 'Tiens' and 'Mon dieu' mingling with the Irish girl's 'Begorrahs'. Miss Theobald clapped her hands over her ears and said sternly, 'Enough! I presume that you are Kitty Flaherty and that the goat belongs to you?'

'Indeed he does, Mam. But 'twas yourself wrote to Mother and gave permission for me to bring him to school,' said Kitty, her merry eyes earnest for a moment.

'But I did nothing of the sort,' said the head, looking puzzled. 'I am afraid, my dear, that there has been some kind of mix-up.'

'Did Mother not write and ask you if I might bring my pet goat to school with me?' asked Kitty, looking crestfallen.

'I don't recall any such letter,' replied Miss Theobald. 'One moment, please.'

Miss Theobald went off to her study, returning moments later with a sheet of paper in her hand. Looking rather dismayed, she said, 'This is the only letter I have received from your mother, Kitty. She asks if you might bring a black and white *coat* to school with you – or so I thought! I believed that she was making enquiries about the clothes you were allowed to bring to school, and replied that this would be all right for your leisure time.'

'Ah, that would be Mother's handwriting,' said Kitty

blithely. 'Sure and it's dreadful! You see, Mam, if you look closely you can just see a little tail on the g there.'

Then McGinty snatched the letter from the astonished Miss Theobald's fingers and, with a very droll expression on his face, began to eat it! The watching girls were in absolute fits of laughter. Tears streamed down Doris' cheeks, while Carlotta held her sides. Even Jenny and Barbara, the two dignified sixth formers, held their hands tightly across their mouths to stop themselves laughing out loud.

'You bad fellow, McGinty!' cried Kitty, though her eyes twinkled. 'What's to be done with you? I'm very sorry, Miss Theobald, but you can see that he won't cost much to feed, for he'll eat anything.'

Miss Theobald could also see that little Kitty Flaherty was going to be quite a handful! But there was something about the naughty, merry little girl that one just couldn't help liking. Hiding a smile, the head said, 'It appears that we have no choice but to accept McGinty as a member of St Clare's. You are responsible for him, Kitty, and if he causes any trouble I shall have to contact your parents and ask them to take him away. You are only to see him during break times and after school, and he is not to disrupt your lessons in any way. Now I suggest you go along to the gardener and he will find McGinty a home in the old stables.'

'Ah, bless you, Mam!' said Kitty, beaming at the head mistress. 'You'll not regret this, I promise you.'

'I hope not,' answered Miss Theobald, smiling back.

'And, Kitty, it is customary to address the mistresses by their names rather than as Mam.'

'Sure and I'll remember that, Mam,' Kitty said happily. 'Come on, McGinty, me boy, let's find you a home.'

Miss Theobald and Mam'zelle, who was still muttering disapprovingly, walked back to the school together and the crowd that had gathered around Kitty began to disperse, until only the third formers were left.

'Hallo there!' said Bobby with a grin. 'Well, you've certainly made a spectacular entrance.'

Kitty grinned back and Janet said, 'Let's help you get McGinty settled in. I'm Janet Robins, by the way, head of the third form. This is Amanda Wilkes, another new girl. Then we have Bobby Ellis, Hilary Wentworth, Isabel O'Sullivan and her cousin Alison. Doris and Carlotta you've already met, of course.'

'O'Sullivan,' repeated Kitty, looking at Isabel with interest. 'Would you be after having a bit of the Irish in you?'

'Yes, Alison's father and mine were both born in Ireland,' said Isabel with a smile. 'What part are you from, Kitty?'

'Ah, the most beautiful little village called Kilblarney,' sighed Kitty wistfully. ''Tis a little bit of heaven on earth. My parents have had to move to London for a little while, because Father – he's a writer, you see – needs to do some research for his latest book. And the big city wouldn't have suited young McGinty here at all, for he's a country boy. It wouldn't have suited me either, for that matter, so I'm afraid you're stuck with the pair of us for the next term.'

The girl's Irish lilt was most musical and quite fascinating to listen to, and Janet said, 'Well, we won't mind that at all. In fact, it's a pity you can't stay longer. I've a feeling we're going to have some fun with you, Kitty Flaherty!'

3

The deputy head girl

The third formers all had to report to Matron and be allocated dormitories. They were rather surprised – and not too pleased – to find that, instead of having two dormitories between them, extra beds had been squeezed into one dormitory and they were all in together.

'I say, this is going to be a bit of a crush!' complained Hilary. 'And it means that none of us will be able to get away from Mirabel's snoring.'

Mirabel Unwin, who had just arrived with her quiet little friend, Gladys Hillman, pushed Hilary playfully. 'I wonder who's having the dorm next door?' she said. 'It certainly seems odd, cramming us all in here like sardines.'

It was Janet who found out the reason for this. While the others showed Kitty and Amanda round the school before tea, she, as head of the form, had to go and see Miss Theobald. She felt extremely nervous as she knocked on the door, a most unusual thing for the bold Janet. Normally she was daring enough for anything, but she was well aware of the honour of being head of the form, as well as the responsibilities it would bring.

Miss Theobald, however, put her completely at ease, smiling her most charming smile and inviting the girl to sit down.

'Well, Janet, this is a very important term for you,' she began. 'I feel confident that you will do your best to be a good head girl.'

'I certainly will, Miss Theobald,' said Janet, feeling very proud indeed.

'I am afraid that you will be coping in somewhat difficult circumstances this term,' the head went on. 'You will have already noticed that all the third formers are to be together in one dormitory instead of two?'

'Yes, and I'm afraid some of the girls aren't too pleased about it,' said Janet, with her usual honesty.

'I can understand that,' said Miss Theobald. 'But it is purely a temporary measure. You see, there is some building work taking place at the moment in the second form's quarters. Their dormitories and common-room are really far too small and are being extended. Obviously it is quite impossible for the girls to use those rooms while work is going on, so the only solution is for them to use one of the third-form dormitories. They will also be sharing your common-room for a while.'

Janet felt most dismayed at this. The second formers weren't a bad crowd on the whole, but the third certainly wouldn't want them sharing in any of their secrets.

'I realise that it's going to be rather cramped and uncomfortable for a while,' said Miss Theobald. 'But the builders have assured me that they will complete the work as soon as possible. In the meantime I can only ask you all to be patient and do your best to get along together.'

Janet responded with a polite 'Yes, Miss Theobald', but she wasn't looking forward to breaking the news to the others that they would have to share their common-room with a lot of noisy, unruly second formers!

The rest of the third form, meanwhile, had finished giving the new girls the 'Grand Tour', as Doris called it, and were pleased when the bell rang for tea.

'Good, I'm starving,' said Hilary. 'Hope it's something nice!'

'I've forgotten the way to the dining-room already,' said Amanda, looking rather forlorn. 'There's so much to remember, I don't think I'll ever find my way around.'

'I'll see to it that you don't get lost,' laughed Isabel, taking her arm. 'Actually I'm feeling at a bit of a loose end myself, without Pat here to turn to.'

'Oh yes, you mentioned someone called Pat earlier,' said Amanda. 'Who is she – your friend?'

'She's my twin,' answered Isabel. 'But she broke her arm and won't be back for a while. You simply can't imagine how queer it is being back at St Clare's without her, because Pat and I do absolutely everything together.'

Amanda was rather sorry to hear this, for she had taken a great liking to Isabel and had hoped that she might become her best friend.

Just then Bobby called out, 'I say, Kitty, where do you think you're going?'

Kitty, who had wandered off towards the big front door, turned and said, 'Why, to check on McGinty. The poor fellow's probably feeling a wee bit lonely on his own in the stables.'

'Well, do be quick or you'll get into a row for being late,' said Hilary. 'Here, Bobby, perhaps you had better go with her to make sure that she doesn't spend all night in the stables with McGinty.'

'Kitty's quite potty about that goat,' chuckled Doris as Bobby and the little Irish girl went outside. 'If the dorm wasn't so overcrowded I bet she'd ask Miss Theobald if he could sleep in there with her!'

McGinty seemed perfectly content where he was, however. Really, he was almost like a dog, thought Bobby, watching in amusement as he wagged his stumpy tail when his mistress approached. He allowed Bobby to pet him too, gently butting her hand and nibbling at the sleeve of her blazer.

'He's awfully sweet,' said Bobby, as she and Kitty walked back to the school. 'You're jolly lucky that Miss Theobald allowed him to stay.'

'Sure, Bobby, I'm always lucky!' said Kitty with an impish smile, her bright eyes twinkling merrily.

A moment later, though, it seemed as though Kitty's luck might have run out, for Margaret Winters was standing at the door of the dining-room. In her hand was a notebook, in which she was busily jotting down the names of all latecomers.

'You two are almost ten minutes late,' she said coldly

to Kitty and Bobby. 'I shall be giving out lines to anyone who is late more than once a week.'

'Sure and I thought that nice, fair girl I met earlier was head girl, not you,' said Kitty, meeting the bigger girl's cold, violet eyes with an innocent stare.

'I've already had to tick you off once today for being insolent,' snapped Margaret. 'Not a very good start for a new girl. And, for your information, Miss Theobald has just made me deputy head girl. Jennifer is very busy with her duties as Games Captain, so she needs someone to assist her.'

And didn't that gladden her spiteful, self-important nature, thought Bobby in dismay. The girl simply couldn't imagine what had made Miss Theobald pick Margaret, for she was everything a head girl shouldn't be, and would be sure to use her power wrongly. And Bobby was quite right, for at that moment Alison – who, as usual, had spent far too long doing her hair – came along and said breathlessly, 'I'm terribly sorry that I'm late, Margaret. I say, I've just heard about you being deputy head girl and I think it's simply marvellous.'

'Why, thank you, Alison,' said the top former, with her attractive smile. 'Go on in now, while there's still some food left.'

'She didn't write Alison's name in the book!' fumed Bobby, as she and Kitty made their way to their table. 'Talk about favouritism!'

'Sure and that one wants taking down a peg or two,' said Kitty, with a thoughtful gleam in her eye.

Strangely enough, Margaret was thinking exactly the same thing about the little Irish girl. She was still smarting over the way Kitty had cheeked her earlier, in front of the whole school, and was determined to get her own back. Little Miss Flaherty had better watch her step!

As Miss Adams, the third-form mistress, was not due back until late that evening, Mam'zelle was at the head of the table and she beamed round, saying happily, 'Ah, how good it is to see everyone back again, all of you refreshed after your break and ready to work hard – especially at your French.'

'If we manage to get any studying done,' said Janet ruefully, deciding that this was as good a time as any to break the bad news to the others. Quickly she explained to them about having to share their common-room with the second form, unsurprised at the outcry that followed. Amanda felt particularly upset, saying dismally, 'Blow! That means I shall have to spend my free time with Helen after all.'

'I daresay we shall get along with most of them all right though,' said Isabel. 'They're a pretty decent lot.'

'Yes, but some of them can be a bit rowdy,' pointed out Hilary.

'Well, we shall just have to sit on them good and hard,' said Janet firmly. 'After all, we are senior to them and it is our common-room.'

'This isn't much of a start to the term,' Doris said glumly. 'Crammed into one dormitory, having to share our common-room and, to top it all, Margaret Winters as deputy head girl.'

'Miss Theobald is usually such a good judge of character,' said Carlotta with a puzzled frown. 'I can't think what possessed her to choose Margaret.'

'Well, you can't deny that she has an air of authority,' sighed Bobby. 'Kitty and I have already fallen foul of her! And she puts on a very different manner for the mistresses from the one she uses with us small fry. They can't seem to see through her at all and think she's just too wonderful for words.'

'What is this you are talking about?' demanded Mam'zelle, who had only caught a few words and hated to be left out.

'Oh, we were just discussing Margaret Winters, Mam'zelle,' said Isabel.

'Ah yes, the dear Margaret,' said the Frenchwoman. 'What a fine deputy she will make. So just and fair!'

'See what I mean?' muttered Bobby under her breath. 'She's pulled the wool right over Mam'zelle's eyes.'

'I agree, Mamzelle,' said Alison raptly, glancing over at the sixth-form table, where Margaret was now seated. 'I think that Margaret will do a super job.'

'Trust Alison,' said Bobby scornfully. 'I did think she had learned some sense after all that business with Fern last term, but she still has to find someone to trot round after like a little dog.'

Fern had been a new girl the previous term, whom Alison had made friends with. But she had caused a lot of trouble for the third and left St Clare's under a cloud at the end of term.

Some of the girls had begun to yawn during tea and they were all glad when bedtime came, tired out after their long journeys and the excitement of the first day back at school. But, thanks to the cramped conditions, getting ready for bed proved to be quite a task!

'Hi, Mirabel, get your elbow out of my face!' protested Doris.

'Alison, those are *my* pyjamas you're putting on,' said Gladys, snatching them back. 'Yours are under the bed, for some reason!'

'Ow, that's my foot you're treading on, Doris!' cried Kitty. 'Sure and McGinty would feel quite at home in here, for it's like a farmyard!'

Isabel caught Amanda's eye and the two of them laughed.

'Settling in OK?' asked Isabel in her friendly way.

'Yes, everyone's been so kind to me,' said Amanda. 'I really think I'm going to like it here.'

'Good,' said Isabel, pleased at this praise of her beloved St Clare's. But she wasn't quite so pleased a few moments later, when Amanda took the bed next to hers, which she had been planning to save for Pat. It seemed mean and unfriendly, though, to ask the new girl to move, especially as she and Isabel had been getting on so well together. Oh well, Amanda seemed a reasonable girl, and no doubt she would agree to move when Pat came back.

'Goodnight, Isabel,' whispered Amanda.

'Goodnight,' Isabel whispered back.

'No more talking now,' came Janet's voice through the darkness. No one really felt like talking anyway, most of the girls falling asleep immediately.

Isabel, drifting pleasantly off, realised that, although her twin was still very much in her thoughts, she didn't feel at all gloomy now. How could she, when there was a whole new term to look forward to, and people like Kitty and Amanda to get to know? It was just impossible to be down in the dumps for long at St Clare's.

Isabel makes a friend

There was so much to do that the first few days of term simply flew by. There were timetables to make, new books to give out and a hundred and one things. Amanda settled in well, though she seemed to find some of the lessons difficult and, while she worked hard, never got very good marks. She seemed to attach herself particularly to Isabel, and Isabel had mixed feelings about this. She liked Amanda enormously and it was very nice to have someone to talk to and share a joke with whilst her twin was away. Yet she couldn't help feeling that she was being disloyal to Pat.

'What nonsense!' scoffed Janet, when Isabel mentioned this to her. 'As if anyone could ever come between you and Pat. I'm sure she's delighted to think that you're not moping about without her. Besides, we've only been back a few days and you've already written to her twice, so she's hardly likely to take it into her head that you've forgotten her!'

So Isabel, reassured by Janet's common-sense words, was able to relax and enjoy her new friendship with Amanda.

Kitty, too, settled down in her own way.

'Although perhaps settled isn't the right word,' remarked Bobby, when she and some of the others were discussing the new girls one day. 'Kitty's so restless and mischievous that she seems positively *un*settled!'

The third had quickly taken the little Irish girl to their hearts, for she was a real character – warm-hearted, fun-loving and very funny in a completely natural way. Kitty didn't have a particular friend of her own, but she didn't seem to want or need one, mixing quite happily with all of the girls. She had absolutely no shyness in her nature and could chatter nineteen-to-the-dozen with almost anyone.

'No wonder Kitty doesn't have a special friend,' remarked Carlotta shrewdly. 'She would be just too much for one person! Her personality is so big that she needs to spread it around everyone.'

Most of the mistresses couldn't help liking Kitty either, though she drove them to distraction at times. As Miss Adams said, she could work well enough when she chose to – it was just a pity that she didn't choose to more often! The girl had a habit of staring out of the window, a dreamy and angelic expression on her face. But as Miss Adams had swiftly learned, the more angelic Kitty looked, the more mischief she was likely to get up to!

'Kitty!' the mistress would say sharply on these occasions. 'Have you listened to a single word that I have been saying?'

'I have and all, Mam,' Kitty would reply solemnly.

'Sure, me eyes might be out there in the garden, but me ears are in here all right.'

Then Miss Adams would shake her head in despair, while the rest of the form struggled to contain their giggles.

Mam'zelle – who as well as being the kindest-hearted mistress in the school was also the most hot-tempered – frequently became exasperated with Kitty too. The Irish girl would make no attempt at a French accent, and the language, spoken in her soft Irish brogue, sounded very funny indeed to the other third formers. Unfortunately, Mam'zelle did not agree with them.

'Ah, Keety! Never have I taught a girl as stubborn as you!' she would cry. 'The poor Doris, now she is slow, but at least she makes an effort. You, though, will not even try! You are as stubborn as that goat of yours!'

'Why, 'tis donkeys that are stubborn, Mam'zelle, not goats,' Kitty would reply, her eyes twinkling, and the Frenchwoman's wrath would descend on her auburn head.

'You'll drive Mam'zelle too far one day,' warned Doris, after a lesson which had almost reduced Mam'zelle to tears. 'Honestly, Kitty, I thought my French accent was bad, but you take the biscuit.'

Then the Irish girl astounded everyone by reciting a few lines of the French poem they had been learning, in rapid, perfectly accented French.

'Kitty, you fraud!' exclaimed Amanda. 'Your accent is the best in the class!'

'But why have you been pretending that you're no good at French all this time?' asked Carlotta, perplexed.

'Sure and I like to see old Mam'zelle fly into a paddy,' answered Kitty with a broad grin. 'It brightens up the lessons no end.'

'Well, you certainly brighten up life at St Clare's,' chuckled Bobby. 'I thought I was cheeky and don't care-ish but, my goodness, you can teach me a thing or two, Kitty!'

The person who came down hardest on Kitty was Margaret Winters. She would pull the girl up over the slightest misdemeanour, even something as trivial as running in the corridor, or having a crooked tie, and would dole out a punishment. The other third formers grew most indignant on Kitty's behalf.

'It's most unfair!' cried Hilary. 'She's doing exactly what a deputy head girl shouldn't – using her position to vent her own personal feelings of spite.'

'Never mind, Kitty old girl,' said Doris. 'I'll do half of those lines for you. My handwriting is a bit like yours – untidy!'

'Ah, you're a good friend, Doris,' said Kitty, handing the girl a sheet of paper.

'Margaret really ought to be reported to Jenny for this,' said Isabel. 'I'm sure she would put a stop to her persecuting poor Kitty.'

'Now, Isabel, don't you go worrying your head about me,' said Kitty, in her usual relaxed manner. She never seemed to get upset about anything, and the girls had yet to see her lose her temper. 'Telling tales isn't my way.'

There was a certain roguish look in Kitty's eye that made Gladys ask curiously, 'And just what is your way, Kitty?'

'Why, I'm thinking that if Margaret is going to punish me over these silly little things, then I may as well do something to really earn the punishment,' answered Kitty.

'Just what do you have in mind?' asked Mirabel, much amused.

'Nothing – yet,' replied the girl. 'But I'll come up with something, to be sure.'

With Kitty in the class the third was a very lively and exciting place to be that term. There was only one fly in the ointment – and that was the second formers. The girls really did find sharing a common-room with them very trying. They talked long into the night after lights-out too, and the sound came through the wall of the third form's dormitory, keeping them awake.

At last Janet lost her temper and got out of bed one night, going to the second-form dormitory and flinging open the door. The second formers fell silent at once, afraid that it was a mistress who stood there, and Janet snapped, 'Well, that's the quietest you've been all night! For goodness' sake, shut up and let us get some sleep! We third formers are tired, even if you lot aren't!'

Without giving the errant second formers a chance to speak up for themselves, Janet shut the door with a slam and went back to her own bed, hoping that her outburst would do the trick.

Sure enough, there wasn't another peep out of the second formers that night and the following morning, when Janet came out of the dormitory, she found Grace, their head girl, waiting for her.

'Sorry about last night, Janet,' said the girl, rather sheepishly. 'It won't happen again, I promise you.'

'Well, I'm glad to hear it,' said Janet frankly. 'I'm sorry that I had to blow up at you like that, but while we're all living together so closely it's important that we consider one another's wishes and feelings. Anyway, so long as it doesn't happen again we'll say no more about it.'

Isabel had a letter from Pat that morning, and she read parts of it out to the third formers at the breakfast table.

'She sends you all her love and says she can't wait to come back,' said Isabel. 'Kitty, she's absolutely longing to meet you – and McGinty, of course.'

'Tell her that we all miss her when you write back, won't you?' said Hilary.

'I will,' replied Isabel. 'I'll try and write the letter at lunchtime, then I can post it this afternoon.'

'I should,' said Carlotta gravely. 'It must be at least two days since you last wrote. Poor Pat must be feeling quite neglected!'

The others laughed – all except Amanda, who was strangely quiet. She was feeling rather put out, because Isabel's twin seemed so keen to meet Kitty, yet she hadn't mentioned her, Amanda, at all. In fact this was

Isabel's fault, for she had carefully avoided saying too much about the girl in her letters to Pat, still feeling a little guilty over her new friendship.

Isabel wrote her letter during the lunch break but, just as she was about to go and post it, she was called to Matron's room over the matter of some missing stockings.

'Blow! Matron will keep me for simply ages, and the post is collected in fifteen minutes,' said Isabel in dismay. 'I did so want to get my letter off today.'

'I'll take it for you,' offered Amanda, holding out her hand. 'I've a letter of my own to post anyway.'

'Would you? Oh thanks, Amanda, you're an angel.' So Isabel handed over the letter and went off to see Matron, while Amanda dashed off to the postbox, which was just outside the school gates. She posted her own letter to her mother, then, just as she was about to put Isabel's into the slot, she stopped, looking thoughtfully at the letter in her hand. Things would be different between Isabel and herself once Pat returned to school, she thought. Twins were so close that she was bound to be pushed out, and Amanda wasn't looking forward to that at all. She liked Isabel so much – how she wished that she didn't have a twin! Then an idea came into her mind. Suppose Pat didn't receive Isabel's letter? She would be sure to think that her twin was settling down at school without her. And if Amanda could intercept any further letters from Pat to Isabel, then Isabel would begin to think that her twin was behaving coldly towards her, and perhaps a rift between them would open up. Amanda shook herself. She couldn't do such a thing – it was wicked! But was it really so wicked to want to keep a friend, whispered a little voice in her head. She knew, from listening to the others, that Pat was extremely popular, and she would soon find someone else to chum up with. She had to make a decision quickly, for here was the postman cycling along the road on his way to empty the box. Hastily, her fingers trembling, she stuffed Isabel's letter into the pocket of her blazer and slipped back in through the school gates.

How guilty she felt later, when Isabel asked, 'Did you remember to post my letter, Amanda old girl?'

'Of course, Isabel,' she answered, quite unable to look her friend in the eye for fear that Isabel would see the guilt on her face.

Two days later another letter arrived for Isabel, and Amanda, who came down to breakfast before the rest of her form, saw it lying next to the girl's plate. She looked round swiftly to make sure that no one was watching, then slipped it quickly into her pocket, turning red as she did so. How she hated doing this! Yet somehow she couldn't seem to stop herself.

5

Alison makes an enemy

On the following afternoon, which was a Saturday, the third form had the luxury of having their common-room all to themselves while the second form were out on a nature walk.

'Isn't it nice to be able to spread ourselves out a bit, instead of feeling so overcrowded,' said Carlotta, stretching out on a sofa.

'I'm just glad to get away from that beastly stepsister of mine,' said Amanda with feeling. 'Stuck-up little madam!'

Janet looked at the girl sharply. Amanda and Helen were the cause of a lot of ill feeling and tension when the two forms were together in the common-room. Most of it was Helen's fault, for she would usually start things by making some sly, sarcastic remark at her stepsister's expense. Then Amanda would retaliate, and it would end with the two of them having a full-scale row, until the head girls intervened to calm things down. It really was most unfair on everyone else, and extremely trying.

There were other things which caused problems too, such as one form wanting to listen to the radiogram, whilst the other wanted to play a gramophone record, or the second formers getting to the common-room first and bagging all the most comfortable seats. It really was a very unsatisfactory situation. Which made it all the more enjoyable now for the third form to have the room to themselves, and they were determined to make the most of it.

'Let's have a dance,' cried Doris, jumping up from her seat and going to the gramophone. Moments later a lively dance tune filled the air, and the girls leapt to their feet. Everyone was in stitches watching Kitty capering about doing a comical Irish jig, when the door opened and Margaret Winters entered. Immediately Kitty stopped dancing, and Gladys hurriedly turned the gramophone down.

'Oh!' said Margaret blankly. 'I was looking for Helen Wilkes of the second form. It's her turn to do my jobs this week.'

It was the custom at St Clare's for the first and second formers to wait on the top-form girls and do their little jobs, such as lighting fires in their studies or making their tea. The third formers all felt thankful that their turn at doing this was behind them and they could now look forward to the time when they were top formers and it would be their turn to be waited on.

'The second formers are all out on a nature walk, Margaret,' Janet said in a coolly polite tone. 'I'm afraid you'll have to get someone from the first form to help you out.'

Margaret didn't look too pleased at this, and Alison

piped up, 'I'd be more than happy to do your jobs for you, Margaret.'

'Why, Alison, that is kind of you!' said Margaret, with her most charming smile. 'Are you quite sure that you don't mind?'

'Oh no!' said Alison, looking worshipfully up at the older girl. 'It will be my pleasure.'

'Sure and that cousin of yours is completely mad,' Kitty remarked to Isabel, when the door had closed behind Margaret and Alison.

'I'll say she is!' agreed Bobby. 'Golly, when I think of the fuss Alison used to kick up about doing the older girls' jobs when she was in the first form – and now that she doesn't have to do it she goes and volunteers!'

'She wouldn't have volunteered if it had been anyone but Margaret,' said Isabel with a grin. 'I don't know why Alison persists in thinking that she's absolutely wonderful, but it's clear that she does!'

'Well, Alison's welcome to Margaret as far as I'm concerned,' said Doris with a grimace. 'Horrid creature! Anyway, why are we wasting a free afternoon talking about her? Turn that gramophone up, Mirabel, and let's have some fun!'

Alison was gone for simply ages, and it was obvious from the blissful expression on her face when she returned that she had had a wonderful time. 'I've been having a chat with Margaret in her study,' she said, rather smugly. 'She really is nice once you get to know her. Look, she gave me this hairslide too, and we've agreed that I'm going to do her jobs all the time from now on.'

'Alison, you are silly,' said Hilary, exasperated. 'Can't you see that Margaret is just making use of you?'

'She is not!' retorted Alison indignantly, turning red. 'In fact she refused my offer at first and I had to talk her into agreeing to it.'

'More fool you,' said Janet scornfully. 'I don't think Miss Adams will be too pleased about it either.'

'What I do in my free time has nothing to do with Miss Adams,' said Alison stiffly. 'I just feel thrilled and terribly honoured that Margaret enjoys my company so much.'

The others gave up. As Bobby said later, there was no doing anything with Alison once she had decided to make a slave of herself for someone. Little did the third form realise that Alison's adoration of Margaret was to lead to a bust-up between them and the second form.

Helen, whose turn it had been to do Margaret's jobs, went straight to the sixth former's study when she returned from her nature walk. She, like Alison, greatly admired the girl and enjoyed working for her. 'Sorry I couldn't come earlier, but we had to go on a nature walk,' she explained rather breathlessly. 'I can stay now, though, and do whatever you want me to. Would you like me to put the kettle on?'

'That's all right,' said Margaret off-handedly. 'Alison O'Sullivan has already done everything. She'll be coming permanently from now on, so I shan't be needing you again, Helen.'

Margaret far preferred Alison's kind of admiration to Helen's. Alison was quite happy to sit in open-mouthed, adoring silence while Margaret talked about herself, speaking only to put in a remark like 'Oh, Margaret, how wonderful!' or 'Oh, Margaret, how clever of you!'. Helen, on the other hand, was far too conceited and full of herself to really worship anyone else whole-heartedly, and was far too fond of talking about her own talents and achievements for Margaret's liking.

The second former felt both angry and humiliated now, as she recalled how she had boasted to the others about how friendly she was becoming with Margaret. How they would laugh when they learned that she had been cast aside in favour of that silly Alison O'Sullivan. Well, Helen was certainly going to tell Alison what she thought of her!

The common-room was extremely crowded that evening, the girls engaged in various activities. Isabel and Amanda were doing a jigsaw together, while Hilary and Janet pored over a crossword. Grace settled down with some embroidery, and others read, listened to the radiogram, or just chattered. Suddenly the door burst open and Helen stalked in, a scowl on her face.

'I say, what's up with you?' asked Harriet of the second form, looking at her in surprise.

Helen ignored her, walking straight over to Alison. 'Well!' she exclaimed, her hands on her hips. 'I just hope that you're pleased with yourself, Alison O'Sullivan!'

'Whatever do you mean?' asked Alison, completely taken aback and quite unable to imagine why Helen was so angry with her.

'Don't put on that innocent expression with me!' snapped Helen. 'It doesn't fool me one little bit. You know what you've done, you mean beast! *I* was supposed to be doing Margaret's jobs for her, but you had to go behind my back and start sucking up to her.'

Now Alison was an extremely gentle-natured girl, who hated rows of any kind. But she certainly wasn't going to let this second former – and a new girl at that – get away with speaking to her so rudely.

'How dare you!' she said, getting to her feet. 'Just who do you think you are talking to?'

Helen, who had thought that Alison would be quite unable to stand up for herself, was most astonished at this, and shrank back, looking alarmed.

'If Margaret doesn't want you around any longer, I'm sure it's no wonder,' went on Alison. 'Your conceited, stuck-up ways are quite unbearable.'

The whole of the second and third form were gathered round now, watching with bated breath, and Amanda, thrilled at seeing that beastly stepsister of hers in a row, called out, 'That's it, Alison! You tell her!'

'Mind your own business!' shouted Helen, turning on Amanda. 'This is between Alison and me. If it isn't just like you to come sticking your nose in!'

Janet, who had been listening to all this in growing

anger, now pushed her way to the front of the group of girls that were gathered round Alison and Helen, her face quite white with fury. 'I've heard enough of this!' she cried, glaring at Helen. 'How dare you speak to third formers in this way? I insist that you apologise at once!'

Helen, who was secretly a little afraid of the sharp-tongued Janet, turned pale and was almost prepared to back down.

Then Grace came forward and said sharply, 'Now look here, Janet, you might be head of the third form, but *I* am head of the second and it's up to me to tick Helen off, not you!'

'Then do it!' snapped Janet, rounding on Grace at once. 'What's the use of being head girl if you can't keep your form in order.'

This really wasn't very fair, for Grace was a very good head girl, but Janet was in such a rage now that she didn't care what she said. Poor Grace looked most upset and there were angry mutterings among the second formers.

'Honestly, you kids!' said Janet scornfully. 'You really ought to be in kindergarten, the way you behave sometimes.'

'Well, Janet, to hear you talk anyone would think that you were in the sixth form, not just the third,' Grace retorted. 'You're only a year older than us, after all, and you really have no right to order us around.'

'Yes, and you third formers are fine ones to accuse *us* of behaving like kids,' put in Harriet, eager to stick up for her form. 'Just look at some of the pranks Kitty plays! And as for Carlotta, why, Jenny Mills had to tick her off for turning cartwheels on the playing field the other day. If that isn't childish I'd like to know what is!'

This was a mistake, for Carlotta, who was half Spanish, had a very fiery temper indeed. She walked over to the unfortunate Harriet, shaking her fist in the girl's face and raging, 'Who are you to criticise my behaviour? Do it again and I will slap you!'

Hilary, seeing that things were rapidly getting out of hand, took Carlotta's arm and pulled her away, while a shaken Harriet retired into the background. It was at this point that the door opened and Miss Jenks, the second-form mistress, appeared. The girls, intent on their quarrel, didn't even notice her at first, as insults and accusations continued to fly back and forth. At last Miss Jenks raised her voice and shouted, 'What on earth is going on in here?'

Everyone fell silent at once, looking most dismayed to see the mistress standing there.

Janet cleared her throat. 'We – er – we were just having a slight disagreement, Miss Jenks.'

'A *slight* disagreement? It sounded as if war had broken out!' said Miss Jenks, obviously displeased. 'Do you realise that you can be heard right at the other end of the corridor?'

'Sorry, Miss Jenks,' everyone muttered sheepishly.

'I should think so! Now kindly find a more civilised

way of settling your differences in future,' said the mistress coldly.

Silence reigned once she had left. The quarrel had ended, but the hostility that had sprung up between the two forms was only just beginning. For the rest of the evening it was as though an invisible line had been drawn down the middle of the common-room, with third formers on one side of it and second formers on the other. Janet wondered where it would all end. What bad luck that this beastliness had all boiled up during her term as head girl.

6

The feud

The row was at the forefront of everyone's minds the following day, and the third formers could talk of little else.

'Cheeky little monkeys!' said Bobby indignantly. 'They can't be allowed to get away with this kind of behaviour.'

'Sure and they need to be taught a lesson,' agreed Kitty. 'Fancy them accusing me of playing pranks! Did you ever hear the like? Now, I think we should let McGinty loose in their dormitory.'

'Yes, fancy them accusing you of playing pranks, Kitty,' said Hilary dryly.

'I'm not going to resort to tricks of that kind,' declared Janet suddenly. 'They're silly, childish and . . .'

'Great fun,' put in Bobby.

'Well, they are, of course,' agreed Janet with a grin. 'But the thing is, I don't want them to be able to accuse us of starting anything. I intend to treat the whole situation in an adult and dignified manner. Unless, of course, they try any tricks on us! Then they had better watch out!'

Alison had been particularly upset by the row, and

still felt very sore with Helen. She poured the whole story out to Margaret in the girl's study that afternoon. For once the sixth former didn't mind not being able to talk about herself, for this was just the kind of thing that she loved listening to. If there was trouble between the second and third forms, Margaret might be able to turn it to her advantage in some way. The girl had an extremely spiteful streak in her nature, and she was both shrewd and clever. There might be a way here to get back at that dreadful Kitty Flaherty, and one or two others in the lower forms who had treated her with a lack of respect. So Margaret was extremely interested in what Alison had to say, taking her side against Helen and sympathising with her warmly. Alison, who was a terrible chatterbox anyway, blossomed under this treatment and promised to let Margaret know if the feud went any further.

It was as Alison was leaving the sixth former's study that Jennifer Mills came in, to borrow a book from Margaret. The head girl looked rather surprised to see Alison there and, as the door closed behind her, she said to Margaret, 'What was Alison doing here? Surely she's not in any kind of trouble?'

'No, she's doing my jobs for me this term,' answered Margaret airily.

'But the first and second formers are supposed to do that,' pointed out Jenny, with a frown. 'Alison's a third former.'

Margaret laughed and said, 'My dear Jenny, I can

assure you that I haven't forced Alison into doing anything that she doesn't want to do. She seems to have taken a liking to me and I thought it would be cruel to turn her away.'

Jenny's frown deepened at this. She knew Margaret well, and it was most unlike her to consider the feelings of a mere third former. 'Is it true that there was some sort of bust-up between the second and third forms last night?' she asked. 'Did Alison mention anything about it?'

'Not a word,' lied Margaret, looking surprised. She certainly wasn't going to let the head girl in on any of the lower school secrets Alison shared with her. Jenny was such a goody-two-shoes that she was quite likely to call Janet and Grace to her study and insist that they shake hands and make up. But that wouldn't suit Margaret at all. The girl was already turning over several cunning schemes in her head.

'You know what these kids are like,' she said to Jenny now. 'Probably just a storm in a teacup.'

'I daresay you're right,' agreed Jenny. 'Whatever it was about, I expect that it's all blown over by now.'

But the row hadn't blown over at all. The second and third formers continued to studiously ignore each other in the common-room that evening, but there was an air of excitement among the younger girls, and a good deal of whispering and giggling.

'They're up to something,' murmured Janet to Bobby. 'The question is, what?'

46

The third formers found out at bedtime. Swiftly they changed, brushed their teeth and got into bed. But they didn't get very far, for the girls found that, no matter how they tried, they simply couldn't push their legs down into their beds.

'I say!' roared Bobby. 'The mean beasts have made us all apple-pie beds!'

Then came the sound of laughter from the other side of the wall that separated the two dormitories, infuriating the third formers even more. Bobby, Carlotta and one or two others were all for marching into the second form's dormitory there and then, to give the pranksters a good ragging. But Janet, every bit as furious as they were, said firmly, 'No. Things are bound to get out of hand and we shall end up with some perfectly horrid punishment.'

'You surely aren't suggesting that we ignore it!' cried Mirabel indignantly.

'Shh! Keep your voice down, idiot!' hissed Janet. 'I'm certainly not suggesting anything of the kind. I know I said that we weren't going to resort to childish tricks, but this changes everything. The second form have struck the first blow, and I intend to retaliate! Gather round, everyone, and let's make some plans. And for heaven's sake, let's do it quietly. We don't want them getting wind of what's in store for them. Now, does anyone have any ideas?'

'We could get hold of Helen's books and hide them somewhere,' suggested Amanda rather spitefully. 'Then we could fill her pencil-box with insects, because she's simply terrified of them, and –'

But Janet broke in, to say sharply, 'This isn't just an excuse for you to get back at your stepsister, you know. It's a form feud now, and we're all involved.'

Amanda looked put out, as did Alison, who had rather liked the idea of getting back at Helen for all the mean things she had said to her.

'We could play some sort of trick on Miss Jenks and make it look as if the second form are responsible,' said Bobby thoughtfully. 'She would be simply furious! You know how Miss Jenks prides herself on never letting anyone get the better of her.'

'That's more like it,' said Janet. 'But it would take us a while to plan, and we really need something that we can put into action quickly, so that the second formers know they haven't got away with this.'

The third formers racked their brains, and at last Bobby said, 'Got it! Janet, do you still have that trick ball that your brother sent you last term?'

'Yes, it should be in my locker. Hold on a minute.' Janet sprang down from the bed and rummaged around in her locker for a few moments. 'Here it is.'

The ball that she held up looked much like any other, but as Bobby explained, 'It has a weight inside, which makes it roll round all over the place when it's hit, instead of going in a straight line.'

'And you've thought of a way to trick the second formers with it?' said Gladys.

Bobby nodded, a mischievous grin on her freckled face and, in a low voice, explained her plan to the others. There were many stifled chuckles as she spoke and, when she had finished, Isabel said, 'Bobby, it's a simply marvellous idea! My goodness, I can't wait to see the second formers' faces when we spring this on them!'

'Nor can I,' said Hilary. 'But right now, we'd better make our beds properly and get some sleep, otherwise we shall be too tired to play this wonderful trick tomorrow.'

So the girls sorted out their beds and settled down to sleep, their thoughts pleasant ones. Just wait until tomorrow, you second formers!

The second form had hockey practice the following afternoon and were keen to make a good showing, as Jennifer Mills was coming to watch, and there was a good chance that some of them would be picked for the junior team. The third form, however, had chosen that moment to take their revenge and were quite determined that no one from the second form would be given a place on the team.

Just before practice began, Isabel, Amanda, Gladys and Mirabel slipped into the changing room and removed all the laces from the second formers' hockey boots. 'We'll put them back later,' said Isabel, slipping the bundle of laces into her bag. 'This is just to stir Miss Wilton up – she hates being kept waiting!'

Next Janet and Bobby carried out their part of the

plan. Whilst Miss Wilton, the games mistress, and Jenny were waiting for the second form to emerge from the changing room, Bobby ran on to the field on the pretext of speaking to them about practice times for the third formers. Janet, meanwhile, sneaked up behind them and slipped the hockey ball into her pocket, replacing it with her own very special one!

'What *is* taking those girls so long?' said Miss Wilton, impatiently, to Jenny, glancing at her watch. 'It seems to be taking them ages to get changed.'

The third formers, all of whom had turned out to watch what promised to be a most entertaining practice, grinned and winked at one another. They knew what was taking the second formers so long, but they weren't telling!

At last the second form came running out on to the field, and Miss Wilton heaved an exasperated sigh. 'Grace! Why are you all wearing plimsolls? What has happened to your hockey boots?'

'Our laces have all gone missing,' answered Grace, glaring in the direction of the third form.

'What, *all* of them?' exclaimed the games mistress, in disbelief. 'How can that have happened?'

Grace knew exactly how it had happened, but she said nothing. The St Clare's girls had very strict ideas of honour and, even in the middle of a feud like this, simply refused to sneak.

'Come along, then – we've wasted quite enough time already,' said Miss Wilton, briskly. 'Take your places, girls, and practise shooting at goal.'

Harriet gave the ball a terrific whack that should have sent it straight into the goal. But instead it simply veered round in a big circle and ended up back at Harriet's feet.

Doris gave one of her explosive snorts of laughter, which was fortunately drowned as Miss Wilton called sharply, 'Do stop fooling around! Helen, stop hanging back and trying to make yourself invisible! Come forward and try to hit the ball *somewhere* near the goal.'

Helen detested all games and, as she was not very good at them, always hated coming to the attention of Miss Wilton. She stepped forward reluctantly and gave the ball a feeble tap. It moved forward a few inches, then rolled back to its starting place. Jenny shook her head in despair, while the third formers clutched at one another gleefully as they tried to stifle their giggles.

'What a super trick!' exclaimed Gladys. 'Oh, I say, do look at Grace!'

Grace was only feet away from the goal, and getting the ball in should have been a simple matter. But as soon as her hockey stick touched it, the ball veered sharply to the left and went wide of the posts.

'Well!' said Jenny. 'What a sorry looking bunch! You lot are going to have to pull your socks up if you hope to stand any chance of getting into the team. Extra coaching for all of you!'

Helen, in particular, looked absolutely aghast at this, for the girls had to give up their free time to attend

Jenny's coaching sessions. She scowled fiercely at the third formers, and Amanda chuckled. 'It looks as if my dear stepsister is going to be taking some more exercise, whether she likes it or not.'

'I vote we make ourselves scarce,' said Hilary. 'Miss Wilton keeps looking at us most suspiciously every time we laugh. If we aren't careful we shall give the game away.'

So, reluctantly, the third formers left, congratulating themselves on an extremely successful trick. But, as Bobby said, 'They are sure to try and get back at us in some way, so we shall have to be ready for them. We can't possibly let the second formers get the better of us. The honour of the third is at stake!'

7

An unexpected arrival

'I say, Isabel, have you had any word from Pat lately?' asked Doris one day. 'When is she coming back?'

Isabel shrugged and said rather stiffly, 'Your guess is as good as mine. She hasn't written to me for days.'

Amanda, sitting nearby, overheard this and turned pink. In fact, Pat had written to her twin several times lately, but she had managed to intercept the letters. The girl had also conveniently forgotten to post several of Isabel's letters to Pat as well. But how wretched Amanda felt at seeing poor Isabel looking so down in the dumps.

'Cheer up,' said Bobby. 'I'm sure there's a simple explanation. Perhaps your father has grown tired of writing everything out for her. I wouldn't blame him! He's probably got writers' cramp with the amount of post you and Pat send back and forth.'

Isabel shook her head. 'No, Daddy always sticks by his word and he knows how much those letters mean to me. I think it's Pat who's grown tired of dictating them.'

'Heavens, I hope you and Pat aren't going to fall out,' said Hilary. 'We've quite enough trouble on our hands at the moment with the second formers.'

'Yes, why don't you write to Pat and tell her all about

that?' suggested Alison. 'If that doesn't get a response, nothing will.'

'I don't think I shall bother,' said Isabel, rather huffily. 'If she can't make the effort to write I don't see why I should!'

As it happened, Pat returned to St Clare's the very next day, feeling every bit as put out as Isabel at her twin's long silence. She had written to tell Isabel what time she would be arriving and quite expected a reception committee from the third form. But when she arrived there was no one to greet her at all. It really was most odd, thought Pat, feeling very hurt.

After reporting to Matron, Pat went to the dormitory to unpack. She knew which was Isabel's bed at once, for there was a photograph of their parents on the locker beside it. But the bed next to Isabel's appeared to have been taken, a neatly folded dressing-gown on top of it and some personal belongings on the locker. Pat began to feel very upset indeed. She and Isabel had *always* slept next to one another. What was her twin thinking of to let someone else take her place?

It was as Pat was brushing her hair in front of the mirror that Amanda came in and exclaimed, 'There you are, Isabel! I've been looking everywhere for you. Listen, I had a postal order from Mummy this morning, so I thought I might treat us both to tea in town. It's my turn, as you paid last time.'

Pat stiffened. So, this was the reason Isabel hadn't written for so long! Well, she certainly hadn't wasted much time in making a new friend. Rather coldly, Pat said, 'I'm not Isabel. I'm her twin.'

Amanda turned a little pale. Soon she would discover whether or not her scheme had worked. Taking a deep breath, she said, 'How do you do? I'm Amanda Wilkes, Isabel's friend. I expect she's mentioned me?'

Pat stared at the girl. She seemed pleasant enough, yet Pat disliked her intensely because she had come between her twin and herself. 'No,' she said shortly. 'Isabel hasn't mentioned you at all.'

And with that she swept past Amanda and out of the room. She found most of the third formers in the common-room, though Isabel was not among them, and got an extremely warm welcome.

'Pat! Marvellous to see you again. How are you?'

'You should have let us know you were coming!'

'I say, won't Isabel be pleased! Have you seen her yet?'

'Hallo, everyone,' said Pat, smiling round. 'It's nice to be back. No, I haven't seen Isabel yet, but I did write and tell her that I was coming.'

'Well, how odd that she didn't let on to us,' said Carlotta.

'Isabel's behaviour has been rather odd altogether these past few weeks,' said Pat, with a harsh laugh. 'She hasn't written in simply ages, and now I find out that she's chummed up with this Amanda.'

'This is all jolly queer,' said Janet, looking mystified. 'Isabel says that *you* haven't written to *her*! Obviously there's been a mix-up somewhere. Anyway, the two of you can thrash it out when you get together. Now, do sit down and we'll tell you all the news.'

Pat sat in between Janet and Bobby on the sofa and said, 'Where are the second form? Isabel mentioned in her first letter to me that you were sharing the common-room with them.'

'The poor little dears are having extra hockey coaching,' said Bobby with a grin, and at once launched into the story of the feud. There was other news to catch up on too, then Kitty had to be introduced and the girls insisted on taking Pat outside to meet McGinty. So it was not until teatime that Pat finally caught up with her twin. Isabel was already seated at the table with Amanda when the rest of the third form entered, and she looked up at Pat rather apprehensively.

'So there you are,' said Pat. 'I thought you were having tea in town with your new friend.'

Isabel flushed, stung by her twin's tone. Pat had no right to object to her being friendly with Amanda when she hadn't even bothered to write for ages.

'Amanda found me in the library and told me that you were back,' she answered. 'Naturally I wouldn't go out to tea on your first day back.'

'Well, I suppose that's something,' sniffed Pat. 'You might have come along to the common-room to say hallo.'

'I did, but by the time I got there you had gone,' said Isabel indignantly.

'That must have been when we popped outside to see McGinty,' put in Hilary quickly, anxious to avert a quarrel. 'Pat, do have something to eat. You must be starving after your journey.'

Pat was, so she sat down as far away from Isabel as possible.

Janet pursed her lips. She liked the twins enormously and knew how close they were. What a shame it would be if they fell out over this. It was a very strange business, each of them claiming not to have received the other's letters. Janet began to feel that there was something fishy going on. And as head girl it was her duty to sort it out.

But she had no time to bend her mind to the problem that evening, for the second formers were up to their tricks again. They made sure that they were first in the common-room, and the door was slightly ajar when the third form arrived. Amanda pushed it open – then what a squeal she let out! For the wicked second formers had carefully balanced a bucket of water on top of the door, and Amanda received the contents all over her. The second formers laughed uncontrollably and Helen drawled, 'I always said you were a drip, Amanda.'

'You horrid little beast!' spluttered Amanda, wiping the water from her eyes. 'I bet you were behind this.'

'How could I possibly have known that you would be first through the door?' laughed Helen. 'That was just bad timing on your part.'

Pat had to turn away to hide a smile at this. Naturally she was on her form's side in this feud, but she couldn't help feeling pleased that the person who had received an unexpected shower was Amanda.

'I should go and get changed if I were you,' advised Doris. 'Before Matron or one of the mistresses comes along and catches you in those wet clothes.'

With one last glower in her stepsister's direction, Amanda stormed off and Janet said scornfully, 'Rather a juvenile trick. Still, what can one expect from a bunch of kids?'

Grace flushed angrily, well aware that the tricks she and her form had come up with weren't nearly so ingenious as the one the third had played on them the other day. She wondered what they would come up with next.

Janet was intent on revenge, she and the rest of the form going into a huddle once Amanda returned in dry clothes.

'That idea you came up with, Bobby, for playing a trick on Miss Jenks would be absolutely super,' Janet said.

'Yes, but it's going to be terribly difficult to play a trick under the eyes of Miss Jenks and the whole of the second form,' said Bobby thoughtfully.

'Come on, thinking caps on, everyone, and let's see if we can't come up with something between us.'

'If we could only get the second form out of their classroom for a while we'd have a clear field, so we would,' said Kitty thoughtfully.

'Golly, that would be a fine trick in itself – to make an entire form disappear,' said Hilary. 'I'm afraid it's a bit of a tall order, though.'

'It is that,' agreed Kitty, an impish twinkle in her eyes. 'But not impossible, I'm thinking.'

'Kitty, you've got a plan, haven't you?' said Alison excitedly. 'What is it?'

'Yes, do tell!' begged Amanda.

'Shush now.' Kitty glanced warningly towards the second formers, who were looking across at them most suspiciously. 'I need to think this out a bit. Come to the stables tomorrow morning while I'm giving McGinty his breakfast and I'll tell you what I have in mind.'

'Why the stables, Kitty?' asked Janet, amused and very curious. Knowing Kitty's mischievous, don't-care-ish nature, any trick she came up with was sure to be simply splendid.

'Because there's something in there that I think might be of use to us,' Kitty answered with a grin. 'I'm saying no more now. Just wait until tomorrow morning.'

The third formers were bursting with curiosity when they got to the stables after breakfast the following morning.

'I say, where's Kitty?' asked Doris. 'I do hope she won't be long or we shall be late for English.'

'She'll be here soon,' said Hilary. 'She's just gone to get some scraps from Cook for McGinty.'

Both Kitty and her pet had quickly become firm favourites with the kitchen staff, and the girls often complained jokingly that McGinty was better fed than they were. The third formers had all grown very fond of the little goat, and there was never any shortage of volunteers to feed him, or walk him on his lead, if Kitty was busy. Even Alison, who had been a little afraid of him at first, now loved to pet him, and she stroked his wiry head as everyone waited for Kitty. At last she appeared, carrying a bucket of scraps, which she placed on the ground before McGinty.

'There you are, me boy,' she said gaily, and at once the goat lost interest in the girls, intent on his breakfast.

'Well?' said Isabel impatiently. 'What's this plan of yours, Kitty?'

In answer the Irish girl went into the empty stall next to McGinty's. In it had been dumped old bits of furniture and boxes of all kinds of odds and ends that were no longer wanted. Kitty went to one of the boxes and pulled something out, holding it aloft for the others' inspection.

'What on earth are we going to do with *that*?' asked Bobby, puzzled.

'Sure, Bobby, and we're going to teach the second form a lesson they'll never forget,' replied Kitty cheerfully. 'Gather round and I'll tell you how.'

8

The third form hatch a plot

The object that Kitty held was an old fire bell, very rusty now for it had been in the stables for some time, and Pat asked, 'How are we going to get the second form to disappear from their classroom with that?'

'Ah, we're not, Pat. We're going to get them to disappear from their dorm,' replied Kitty. 'Tricks aren't just for the classroom, you know. You have midnight feasts here, don't you? Well, tonight we're going to play a midnight trick.'

There were gasps of surprise and delight at this. How simply thrilling!

'Go on, Kitty,' said Mirabel eagerly. 'Tell us the plan.'

'Well, at midnight – or thereabouts – one of us will sneak out on to the landing and ring the fire bell,' Kitty explained. 'It still works, but not loudly enough to wake anyone further away, so the only people it will disturb will be the second formers.'

'Then what?' asked Doris, who was jumping up and down in excitement.

'Then the fun really starts,' chuckled Kitty. 'The second formers will follow the fire drill, of course, and go downstairs and out of the side door.'

'But won't they wonder why *we* haven't heard it and aren't taking action ourselves?' said Gladys, with a frown.

'But we will be taking action, Gladys,' answered Kitty. 'We'll put on our dressing-gowns and follow the second form downstairs, all the while acting very surprised and scared. Then, once they've slipped outside, we bolt the door behind them, run back to our dorm, and wait for the person on duty to discover that they're missing.'

'Kitty!' exclaimed Carlotta, delighted. 'It's marvellous!'

'I'm not so sure,' put in Hilary, looking doubtful. 'If Miss Jenks catches the second formers out of bed they'll be in real trouble. And they were decent enough not to sneak on us yesterday morning after hockey practice.'

There were a few murmurs of agreement, and Kitty exclaimed, 'I knew there was something I'd forgotten to mention! You see, I happened to overhear Miss Jenks telling Miss Adams that she would be away tonight, so that nice Jenny Mills is on duty instead.'

'That settles it, then,' said Doris happily. 'Jenny's a decent sort. She'll give the second form a jolly good ticking off, but she won't report them to Miss Theobald.'

'Golly, it will be sport!' said Janet. 'Well done, Kitty. Now come along, everyone, or we shall be late.'

Laughing and chattering, the girls moved away and, as always, Pat turned automatically towards Isabel, so that they could discuss the trick together, forgetting for a moment that there was any coolness between them. Isabel grinned at her twin and opened her mouth to speak. Then, suddenly, Amanda was at her side, taking her arm and saying excitedly, 'My word, what a trick this is going to be! I do like Kitty so much, don't you?' The smile was wiped from Pat's face, replaced by a cold look as she turned her back on her twin and went off to catch up with Hilary. Isabel felt deeply hurt. Why was Pat behaving like this? She was the one who was in the wrong, for not having replied to any of Isabel's letters, and she was being perfectly beastly to poor old Amanda.

Janet noticed this little incident too, and frowned heavily. She had hoped that the coolness between the twins would blow over and they would make up, but instead a real rift seemed to be opening. Janet made up her mind that tomorrow, once this trick was out of the way, she would tackle Pat and Isabel. If she could get to the bottom of this business of the letters perhaps she could bring them together. Being head of the form certainly had its fair share of problems!

Bedtime couldn't come quickly enough for the third formers that evening, though all of them were quite certain they wouldn't get a wink of sleep, spirits high at the prospect of the trick that was to be played. It had been extremely difficult to keep their minds on their work during lessons, and Miss Adams had found it necessary to call several of them to order.

'Doris!' she had barked. 'Why do you keep grinning to yourself in that idiotic way? Do you find my method of teaching maths so amusing?'

Doris, who didn't find maths at all amusing, at once

made her face perfectly serious and said meekly, 'No, Miss Adams.'

'I'm glad to hear it! Now, if Bobby would kindly refrain from whispering to Carlotta and give me her attention also, we might get some work done,' said the mistress dryly.

Bobby had fallen silent immediately, sitting up straight in her seat, and Miss Adams had no further trouble with her class.

Kitty, though, grew extremely restless during French, bringing Mam'zelle's anger upon her.

'Kee-ty!' cried the French mistress, as the little Irish girl gazed out of the window. 'Twice have I asked you to stand up and recite a verse of this so-moving French poem, and twice have you ignored me! What is outside that fascinates you so?'

'Ah, 'tis nothing, Mam,' answered Kitty, her lips twitching humorously. 'I thought I saw McGinty out there, but I must have been mistaken.'

'McGinty?' repeated Mam'zelle, her glasses slipping down her nose.

'My little goat,' explained the girl. 'I could have sworn I saw him in the flowerbed outside the window of the mistresses' common-room.'

'How can this be?' demanded Mam'zelle. 'That goat is in the stables.'

'Sure, but he's a clever one, Mam. If he wanted to slip out and have a taste of those delicious-looking flowers he would find a way.'

Mam'zelle gave a shriek of dismay. The tiny flowerbed was her pride and joy, and she had planted many of the seeds herself, tending them lovingly whenever she had a spare moment.

'This is abominable!' she wailed. 'And you, Kee-ty, *you* are abominable! If that creature has eaten my beautiful flowers I will have him expelled!' With that she rushed from the classroom to go in search of McGinty and, as soon as the door closed behind her, the class exploded into laughter.

'Poor old Mam'zelle,' gasped Amanda, holding her sides. 'Kitty, you're wicked.'

'Yes, and the funny thing is, I was looking out of the window too,' said Carlotta with a grin. 'Yet I didn't see hide nor hair of McGinty.'

'Ah well, I did say I could have been mistaken,' said Kitty, her blue eyes gazing innocently around the class. 'But once old Mam'zelle gets an idea into her head there's no stopping her.'

The others roared. They had needed an excuse to release some of the laughter that was bubbling up inside them, and Kitty had provided it. The third formers chatted happily amongst themselves until Gladys, standing guard by the door, hissed, 'Shh! Mam'zelle's coming back.'

Instantly there was silence, and Gladys scuttled back to her seat as the French mistress entered, her sloe-black eyes fixed angrily on Kitty. 'There was no goat in the flowerbed,' she declared. 'He is safely locked away in the old stables.'

'Ah, that's a relief, Mam,' said Kitty solemnly. 'It's terrible worried I've been.'

'Your worries are just beginning, Kee-ty! Tonight you will learn the French poem, and tomorrow you will recite it to me perfectly, with not one mistake.'

Kitty, who was blessed with an amazing memory and already knew the poem off by heart, bowed her head to hide a smile and answered meekly, 'Yes, Mam.'

'And do not call me Mam!'

Alison was still smiling to herself over this incident when she went to Margaret Winters' study after tea that afternoon. Because they were so angry with Helen, she and Amanda were looking forward to tonight's trick more eagerly than any of the third form.

'You look happy, Alison,' remarked the sixth former pleasantly. 'Is it your birthday or something?'

Alison hesitated. She liked Margaret so much and would have loved to tell her what was going to take place that evening. But as silly as she was, Alison knew that the others would not take kindly to her sharing third-form secrets with a sixth former – especially Margaret. So she muttered something about having got good marks for her English prep and set about boiling the kettle for Margaret's tea. The sixth former, however, wasn't fooled. Margaret was shrewd, and she could sense Alison's excitement. The third formers were up to something, and Margaret badly wanted to know what.

'Sit down and have a cup of tea with me, Alison,' she invited sweetly. 'I've got some chocolate biscuits, too.'

Alison turned quite pink with pleasure, hardly able to stammer out her thanks. What an honour, for a mere third former to be invited to have tea with the deputy head girl! Just wait until she got back to the common-room and told the others – silly little Helen would be green with envy! Alison didn't realise that she was smiling to herself at these pleasant thoughts, but Margaret's sharp eyes noted it and, her voice full of concern, she said, 'I do hope that things are all right between you and Helen now, Alison. I feel simply terrible that I'm the cause of ill feeling between you. But I do enjoy your company so much, and when you offered to carry on doing my jobs I'm afraid I simply couldn't resist saying yes.'

And Alison simply couldn't resist flattery! She beamed with delight as Margaret went on, 'And Helen is so full of herself that I couldn't bear having her around. It's a pity you third formers haven't come up with a plan for taking her down a peg or two.'

Alison bit her lip, longing to tell the older girl about the trick her form was planning for tonight. Margaret was such a wonderful person, so understanding and easy to talk to. It was such a shame that the others couldn't see it. Of course, she could be a little sharp-tongued with people like Kitty and Bobby at times, but they were so disrespectful to her that it was quite their own fault.

Margaret could certainly turn on the charm when she wanted something, and now she gave Alison her most dazzling smile, saying, 'I remember when I was in the third form. My word, what tricks we used to get up to! Of course, I have to behave myself now that I'm a prim and proper sixth former, but I do so enjoy hearing about all your pranks.' Margaret's smile became slightly wistful, and suddenly the strain of keeping her secret became too much for Alison. Before she could stop herself, the girl was pouring out the whole story of the fire bell trick. Margaret listened avidly, her violet eyes sparkling with excitement, and Alison thought how pretty she looked.

'What a simply marvellous trick!' exclaimed the sixth former, when Alison came to the end of her tale. 'You must come along tomorrow and tell me how it went. But now, I'm afraid, I must get on with my prep. Be a dear and clear the table before you go, Alison.'

'Of course, Margaret.' Eagerly the girl jumped to her feet and did as she was told. 'Shall I wash the cups out?'

'Oh no, don't bother about that. I'll do it later.'

Now that Margaret had learned the third form's secret, she wanted Alison out of the way as quickly as possible, for she had a plan of her own. A plan that would get her just what she wanted, as long as she thought it out carefully. As soon as the door closed behind Alison, Margaret went across to a cupboard in the corner of the room and took something out. Then she smiled to herself. The third formers weren't the only ones who were going to enjoy themselves tonight!

A very successful trick

The third formers had planned their trick well. Earlier that day, Mirabel had overheard Jennifer Mills talking to her friend Barbara.

'I don't want to be too late getting to bed, or I shall never get up in the morning! On the other hand, I suppose I'd better make sure that the little beasts aren't planning a midnight feast or something.'

'Yes, some of those second formers are quite a handful.' Barbara had laughed. 'Though I suppose we were just the same at their age! I should check on them soon after midnight, then you can be tucked up in bed by half past twelve.'

Jennifer had agreed that this was a good idea, and Mirabel had raced off to report to the others.

'Well done, Mirabel,' Janet had said. 'We'd better sound the fire bell at ten minutes to twelve. That leaves plenty of time for the second form to get outside.'

'And for us to get back to bed, so that it looks as if we're fast asleep when Jenny comes round,' Isabel had finished with a grin.

At a quarter to twelve the little alarm clock that Carlotta had placed under her pillow went off. The girl sprang from her bed and went round quickly and quietly waking the others. A few girls had been too excited to sleep, but most had dozed off and yawned and stretched sleepily as they sat up.

'Doris!' hissed Carlotta. 'Doris, wake up! We need to get a move on or our trick will be ruined.'

Grumbling to herself, Doris emerged from beneath her lovely warm quilt and groaned.

At last everyone was awake and, shining her torch round, Janet whispered, 'Kitty, have you got the fire bell?'

Kitty nodded and Janet said, 'Good, then let's . . . Amanda, where are you going?'

Amanda, already in dressing-gown and slippers, was heading for the door. She stopped and said, 'I thought we were going to gather on the landing.'

'Not until Kitty has sounded the fire bell! If the second form come out and find us all ready and waiting they'll be very suspicious. We have to act as surprised and scared as they will be.'

'Idiot!' muttered Pat, glaring at Amanda, who flushed.

'Right,' Janet went on briskly. 'Kitty, you know what to do. Everyone else, get into your dressing-gowns and slippers.'

Quietly opening the door, Kitty darted out on to the landing and placed the fire bell in a dark corner. Then she set it ringing and, hands over her ears, rushed back into the dormitory, closing the door behind her.

'My goodness, that sounds dreadfully loud,' said Hilary. 'It'll be a wonder if it doesn't wake the whole building.'

'It won't,' Bobby assured her. 'We're miles away from the rest of the school, and once the second formers are safely out of the way we can stop it.'

Through the wall the girls could hear cries of alarm and bustling noises, then came the sound of a door opening. Winking at the others, Janet went out on to the landing, making her voice very scared as she asked, 'Grace, is that you? You'd better get your form out quickly.'

'They're all ready,' replied the second former, her voice shaking a little. 'Where do you suppose the fire is, Janet? I can't smell any smoke.'

'We don't have time to worry about that now. Let's just concentrate on getting everyone out safely.'

All the St Clare's girls knew the fire drill well, and Grace felt proud of her form as they filed quickly down the stairs, all of them appearing much more calm than they felt. The third formers followed close behind, Janet calling out, 'Unlock the door, Grace, and let everyone out into the garden.'

Grace obeyed, her fingers trembling a little as they slid back the heavy iron bolt. She pulled open the door and the second form made their escape, all of them relieved to be outside. But their relief soon turned to bewilderment, for Carlotta, the first member of the third form to reach the bottom of the stairs, swiftly pushed the door closed behind them, slipping the bolt back into place. Grinning up at her friends, she said, 'Now let's get back to bed. And Kitty, for heaven's sake turn that fire bell off before Jenny gets here.'

Chuckling to themselves, the third formers sprinted back up the stairs, the muffled tones of the second formers following them.

'I say, what's going on?'

'We've been tricked, that's what!'

'The mean beasts! We'll get them for this!'

'Oh no you won't,' thought Janet, a determined smile on her face. No one was going to get the better of the third form while she was head girl! Certainly not a bunch of half-baked kids like the second form.

On the landing Kitty stopped the fire bell and stowed it safely in her bedside locker, and everyone sighed thankfully as the persistent clanging abruptly stopped.

'Are you all right, Alison?' whispered Pat to her cousin, as they slipped back into their beds. 'You've been awfully quiet tonight.'

'I'm fine,' replied Alison, sounding a little subdued. 'Just tired, that's all.' In fact, Alison's conscience was troubling her, and she now wished wholeheartedly that she had never told Margaret Winters about the trick. It had all seemed so *right* earlier, so natural to confide in her. But the others would never forgive her if they knew that she had given away the third form's secret. And to the deputy head girl, of all people! What if Margaret decided to report them to Miss Theobald after all? Alison shifted uncomfortably in her bed, reminding herself firmly that the sixth former had given her word not to sneak. And Margaret would not go back on her word, for she was a decent and loyal person, no matter what the others said! All the same, Alison would be glad when the trick was over. She hadn't long to wait.

Moments later, footsteps could be heard on the landing, and Jennifer's tall, slender figure was silhouetted in the doorway. All was silent until Doris gave a very loud, very realistic snore, grunting to herself as she turned over in bed. Isabel stuffed a corner of the pillow into her mouth to stifle her giggles, but Jennifer seemed perfectly satisfied that all was well and shut the door softly behind her. The third formers lay there with bated breath as she moved on to the second form's dormitory. They heard Jennifer enter, a moment's silence, then an angry exclamation, and the girls sat up in their beds as the head girl's brisk footsteps faded into the distance.

'I bet she's heading for the common-room, to see if they're having a midnight feast,' said Hilary.

'I say, are you absolutely sure Jenny won't wake one of the mistresses?' said Gladys anxiously. 'I know the second form are little beasts, but I wouldn't want to get them into real trouble.'

'Of course she won't,' Bobby assured her. 'Jenny's a good sport. Now, if it had been Margaret Winters who was on duty . . .'

Everyone groaned – except for Alison, whose guilty feelings made her speak out in defence of her idol. 'Why are you all so horrible about Margaret?' she cried, the easy tears starting in her large blue eyes. 'You don't know her like I do, but –'

'We don't *want* to know her!' interrupted Bobby rudely. 'Honestly, Alison, when are you going to take off those rose-tinted glasses of yours and see our dear deputy head girl as she really is?'

Alison opened her mouth to retaliate, but before she could speak Bobby went on, 'She found out that the first form were holding a feast last term and made sure they were caught. The poor things weren't allowed out of the grounds for a fortnight.'

'That was all a misunderstanding!' said Alison hotly. 'Margaret explained it all to me, and what happened was –'

'We know what happened,' said Janet scornfully. 'Your precious Margaret couldn't resist stirring up trouble. And I, for one, don't want to waste any more time talking about her.'

'Hear hear!' put in Isabel. 'Come on, everybody! Jenny's safely out of the way, so let's take a peek out of the window and see what's going on.'

This sounded like an excellent idea, and the third formers scrambled out of bed, padding over to the big window at the end of the room.

'There are the second formers!' said Mirabel, pointing. 'Over by the gardener's shed. My word, don't they look cold!'

The watching girls laughed at the sight of the shivering second formers, all huddled together by the big shed. It was a cold, clear night, the moon lighting the scene beautifully, and Kitty said, 'Sure, it's as good as a play. Let's see if we can hear what they're saying.'

With that she slid the window up a few inches, and the still night air carried the second formers' voices up to the watching girls.

'I'm frozen! What if they leave us out here all night?' Amanda recognised Helen's tearful, high-pitched voice and grinned.

'They wouldn't dare!' said Grace. 'That would be going too far, even for the third form.'

'Suppose Miss Jenks comes along and finds our beds empty?' said Katie fearfully, unaware that the mistress was away for the evening. 'Shall we go and bang on the door?'

'We'll wake the whole school!' said Harriet. 'No, we'll just have to wait until the third formers decide to unlock the door and let us back in. They won't leave us out here too long, I'm sure.' Harriet was trying her best to sound confident, but the listening girls heard the note of uncertainty in her voice.

Then another voice joined the throng outside – a stern, angry voice. 'What on earth are you kids doing out of your beds?' it said, and the second formers almost jumped out of their skins. Jennifer Mills had sneaked around the other side of the shed and crept up on them from behind. 'Well?' she demanded now, folding her arms and glaring at the frightened girls. 'I'm waiting for an explanation.'

'Oh, Jenny, we've been tricked!' began Helen. 'It was those awful –' But she got no further, for Grace elbowed her sharply before she could sneak on the third form.

Bravely, Grace faced up to the head girl and said frankly, 'We're sorry, Jenny. It was . . . it was just a prank that went wrong, and somehow we ended up getting locked out.'

'Are you going to report us to Miss Theobald?' asked Katie, her eyes big and scared looking.

'I ought to,' said Jenny crossly. 'You youngsters deserve –'

But the second formers never found out what they deserved, for two things happened at once. Katie began to cry, and a window overlooking the garden was thrown open. A large, angry head appeared and everyone recognised Mam'zelle's distinctive voice as she cried, 'Who is there? If you are burglars, be warned! I go to call the police!'

The second formers looked at one another in horror and, thinking quickly, Jennifer ushered them into the shadows, putting an arm around the weeping Katie.

'Good old Mam'zelle,' chuckled Doris, enjoying the scene hugely. 'Every time she hears the slightest noise in the night she thinks it's burglars.'

'She won't call the police,' said Janet. 'As long as Jenny can keep those kids quiet and out of sight for a few minutes, Mam'zelle will think she's imagining things and go back to bed.'

At that moment a small movement in the bushes down below caught Alison's eye, but she could see no one. It was probably the school cat on one of his night time prowls. Or perhaps a rat or a mouse! Even from a distance, the thought of rats and mice made Alison shudder, and she stepped back from the window.

Mam'zelle, meanwhile, as Janet had predicted, had grown tired of uttering threats to the empty air and closed the window.

'Right, kids,' said Jenny briskly. 'Make a run for it while the coast is clear and head for the side door. I came out that way, so it should still be unlocked. Go straight up to your dorm and don't stop for anything.'

The second formers didn't need telling twice, sprinting across the lawn until they disappeared from the view of the watching third form, while Jennifer followed at a more dignified pace.

'Show's over,' said Carlotta, closing the window. 'We'd better get some sleep.'

And what a show it had been, agreed everyone. One of the best tricks they had ever played! Simply super!

And Alison felt happier than any of them, breathing a sigh of relief as she listened to the second formers returning to their dormitory. It was over, and Margaret hadn't let her down. The older girl could so easily have interfered and got the whole of the third form into hot water, but she hadn't. For once Alison had been proved right about someone, and it was a very pleasant feeling.

10

A shock for the second form

Following the success of the trick, Janet felt that she could afford to be generous and decided to offer a truce to the second formers. But Grace, angry at being duped, irritable from lack of sleep and still smarting from a painful interview with Jennifer Mills, was in no mood to forgive and forget. 'We're not interested, Janet,' she said coldly. 'Your form made complete idiots out of us last night, and we shan't rest until we've got our own back.'

Janet laughed. 'Just as you like, Grace. But you kids will never get one over on us third formers. We're far too clever for you.'

And it seemed that Janet was right. Helen, finding herself alone in the common-room one morning, decided to steal Amanda's maths book and hide it. But Carlotta came in and caught her in the act, ticking the girl off so fiercely that Helen fled in terror. An attempt to get Kitty into trouble by setting McGinty free also backfired, when the little goat spotted Harriet's French prep sticking out of her satchel and promptly ate it. Finally they made the mistake of trying to play the same trick twice, by balancing a bucket of water on top of the common-room door. The alert third formers spotted it from the corridor and, after a whispered conference, decided to spend the evening at a slide show in the hall. So the second form were left alone to gaze hopefully at the door all evening, a pastime of which they soon grew heartily bored.

'Poor,' said Bobby later, shaking her head gravely. 'Very poor. These youngsters just don't have our ingenuity.'

Grace, who overheard this, simmered with rage and became more determined than ever to get revenge on the third form. She would be seeing her older brother at half-term – perhaps he could come up with an idea.

The third formers were looking forward to half-term. It would be such fun to see parents, brothers and sisters again, and find out what was going on at home. There was great excitement at St Clare's in the few days leading up to the holiday, and the girls found it very hard to sleep the night before.

But, at last, the big day arrived, the entrance hall and the lawn outside thronged with happy, chattering girls as they waited excitedly for their parents to arrive. Pat and Isabel were among them, but they were not so happy as the others. Of course, it would be simply wonderful to see their mother and father again, but things still weren't right between the two of them. So instead of gaily discussing their plans for the day, Pat and Isabel made polite, rather stiff small talk, punctuated by long, awkward silences. It was a situation the twins had never found themselves in before, and it felt most uncomfortable. Fortunately for them, their parents were among the first to arrive. Naturally it didn't take Mrs O'Sullivan long to realise that something was wrong, for she knew her daughters very well indeed. She was extremely dismayed because, although the twins had their squabbles, like all sisters, she had never known them to be so cold and distant towards one another before.

For most of the girls, though, half-term was a very happy time. Carlotta's father and grandmother were unable to come, so she was delighted to be asked out by Kitty, whose parents turned out to be every bit as mad as their daughter. They went for a picnic because, naturally, McGinty had to come as well. The little goat thoroughly enjoyed his day out, being spoiled and petted by the two girls and eating all the leftovers from the picnic.

As Hilary's parents were abroad, Doris invited her to spend the day with her people. They had a simply marvellous time, Mr and Mrs Elward treating the two girls to a slap-up lunch at a restaurant before taking them to see a show.

Amanda's pretty mother and Helen's father, a tall, good-looking man with a humorous face, also turned up, each parent warmly hugging both girls. But Amanda glared furiously at Helen when Mrs Wilkes put an arm round her, while Helen eyed Amanda jealously as she joked with Mr Wilkes. How silly they both were, thought Gladys, walking by arm-in-arm with her own mother. Didn't they realise how lucky they were to have two kind, loving parents?

Alison was happy to see her people again, spending a very pleasant day with them. And, just when she thought things couldn't get any better, she bumped into Margaret Winters, who was showing her parents round the grounds.

'Alison, do come and meet my people,' said the older girl, putting a hand on her shoulder. 'Mummy, Daddy – this is Alison, the girl I was telling you about. She does all my little jobs for me and is an absolute angel!'

Alison turned red, partly from pride and partly because she felt quite over-awed in the presence of this grand-looking couple. Mrs Winters, although perhaps a little over-dressed for the occasion, was the most elegant person she had ever seen, and it was easy to see from whom Margaret had inherited her good looks. She greeted Alison with a polite smile and a regal nod of the head. Mr Winters, who looked most distinguished, was more friendly, shaking Alison's hand and recommending her not to allow Margaret to work her too hard. But his eyes twinkled as he spoke, and it was plain that he adored his daughter. Alison walked away with her head in the clouds, thrilled to think that she was the only member of the lower school who had had the honour of being introduced to the deputy head girl's parents.

But, all too soon, half-term was over and, as the third formers prepared for bed that evening, Doris said glumly, 'Back to the old routine. Why does half-term always seem to fly by so quickly?'

'Cheer up, Doris,' said Bobby. 'We've all had a simply marvellous day. I can't remember when I last enjoyed myself so much.'

'That goes for me, too,' added Hilary, climbing into bed. 'It was jolly kind of you and your people to invite me along, Doris.'

'I wonder if the second half of the term will be as eventful as the first?' mused Janet, sitting up in bed and hugging her knees. 'It's been a strange sort of term so far, what with one thing and another.'

'Yes, it has,' agreed Hilary. 'For my part, I hope things settle down a bit now. I've had quite enough excitement for one term.'

But things weren't about to settle down at all. The third formers, worn out and happy, drifted off to sleep one by one, all of them blissfully unaware of the shock they had in store for them the following day.

It all started with a rumour. 'I say!' exclaimed Amanda, sitting down next to Isabel at breakfast. 'Have you heard about Jenny Mills?'

'What about her?' asked Carlotta, buttering a slice of toast.

'Apparently . . .' Amanda leaned forward over the table and lowered her voice. 'Apparently Miss Theobald has asked her to resign as head girl.' She sat back and folded her arms, waiting expectantly for the reaction to her bombshell. But Amanda was disappointed, as the girls were distinctly unimpressed.

'Nonsense!' said Pat scornfully. 'Miss Theobald thinks the world of Jenny. You've got hold of the wrong end of the stick, Amanda.'

'I'm quite sure I haven't!' retorted Amanda, stung. 'I heard a group of first formers chattering about it in the corridor, and they said –'

'First formers! They're just babies,' said Janet loftily. 'What do they know?'

'I expect someone was pulling their leg, Amanda,' Isabel said. 'And they fell for it.'

'Yes, there are always rumours of some sort or another flying around in a school of this size,' said Hilary. 'And nine times out of ten they turn out to be untrue.'

'Oh,' said Amanda, looking rather crestfallen. Not that she wanted Jennifer to lose her position as head girl, of course, for she liked the top former enormously. But it would have been rather a thrill to be first with the gossip.

The third formers thought no more about Amanda's story until morning break, when Carlotta and Kitty, on their way back from a visit to McGinty, spotted Jennifer and Barbara Thompson walking towards them. Normally the two top formers would have called out a friendly greeting, but today they didn't even notice the younger girls, walking past them as if they simply didn't exist. Both of them wore unusually grave expressions, and Jennifer in particular looked pale and strained, her eyes suspiciously red. Carlotta and Kitty exchanged worried glances.

'It *can't* be true!' Carlotta said, with a frown. 'Why, Jenny is one of the most popular head girls St Clare's has ever had.'

'Of course she is,' said Kitty. 'Don't go worrying yourself now, Carlotta. Perhaps Jenny's had a falling out with one of her friends, or something.'

But by lunchtime the rumour had spread like wildfire. Everyone in the school had heard the story and, reluctantly, a lot of the girls began to believe that it must be true. To make matters worse, there was also a tale going round that Margaret Winters, as deputy head girl, had now been asked to step into Jenny's shoes.

'Can things get any worse?' groaned Doris, her head in her hands.

As it happened, they could – and did. Shortly after tea, Grace was summoned to the head's office. The second formers weren't particularly alarmed by this, as Miss Theobald often sent for the form heads to discuss various matters with them. Besides, like the rest of the school, they were far more worried about the prospect of having Margaret Winters as their head girl.

The atmosphere in the common-room was very subdued that evening, the second and third formers too preoccupied to even bother goading each other. Then Grace came back from her talk with Miss Theobald.

'What did the head want?' asked Harriet, glancing up from her book.

'You've been absolutely ages, and . . . I say! Whatever's the matter, Grace?'

Everyone looked round. Grace was trembling, and as white as a sheet. Through clenched teeth, the girl said, 'She knows. Miss Theobald knows.'

'Knows what?' asked Helen, looking bewildered. 'Grace, what on earth are you talking about?'

'Miss Theobald knows about us being out of our beds last week, and thinks we were up to no good. That's why she's suspended Jenny as head girl, because she knew and didn't report it.' Grace paused and looked round the room, her eyes hard. 'Someone's sneaked!'

A truce – and more trouble

The third formers looked at one another in horror. Never had they guessed for one moment that a simple trick would lead to so much trouble! Tricks were supposed to be fun, but no one felt like laughing now. A perfect hubbub broke out among the second formers.

'Who split on us, Grace? Did the head tell you?'

'Whoever it was is a mean beast! How I wish I could get my hands on her!'

'What's going to happen to us, Grace? Will we be punished?'

'Miss Theobald didn't tell me who the sneak was,' answered Grace angrily. 'And yes, Katie, we're being punished all right. No trips to town for a fortnight. And when Miss Jenks finds out about it, no doubt she'll have a punishment of her own to add too.'

'No!' Janet stepped forward suddenly. 'You won't be punished. I'm going to see the head now, and I'll tell her it was all our fault.'

'That's decent of you, Janet, but you don't have to do that,' said Grace.

'Oh yes I do,' Janet said firmly. 'The third form can't stand by and watch you kids suffer for something we did.' She looked round at her form, and everyone nodded in agreement.

'I'll come with you,' said Hilary.

'And me,' added Isabel.

In the end, the whole form volunteered to go with Janet. Even Amanda, not because she had any real wish to get the second form out of trouble, but because she always followed Isabel's lead.

'We can't all go,' said Janet. 'Miss Theobald will think that she's been invaded! Hilary, you come with me, and the twins.' She grimaced. 'It's not going to be pleasant, so we may as well get it over with.'

Their heads held high, but all of them feeling very nervous indeed, the four girls trooped off to Miss Theobald's office.

The head was looking unusually grave when they entered, saying in her clear voice, 'Well, girls? What can I do for you?'

'It's about the trouble that the second form are in,' began Janet, bravely looking Miss Theobald in the eye, though inwardly she was quaking.

'What has that to do with you, Janet?' asked the head, frowning.

'Well, you see, Miss Theobald, it was all our fault. We found an old fire bell in the stables and set it off as a joke.' Once Janet had begun, the words came tumbling out, and soon Miss Theobald knew the whole story.

'I see,' she said at last, looking very serious. 'Rather a childish and irresponsible trick, Janet.'

The third formers blushed to the roots of their hair and looked at the floor.

'We're truly sorry, Miss Theobald,' said Hilary. 'It was only meant to be a bit of fun.'

'I daresay,' said the head dryly. 'But your bit of fun has led to serious consequences, Hilary. However, I am extremely glad that you have had the courage to own up. I see now that the second formers were not to blame and were, in fact, acting very sensibly in following the fire drill. When you return to the common-room you may tell them that their punishment has been lifted.'

'Yes, Miss Theobald,' said Janet, feeling half relieved and half apprehensive. Relieved because the second formers would not, after all, be punished. And apprehensive because she knew that her own form would not get off so lightly. And she was right.

'As for you third formers, you will receive two punishments,' said Miss Theobald, making the waiting girls' hearts sink even further. 'You will not be allowed to leave the school grounds for a fortnight, and you will also be given an extra thirty minutes prep every evening for the next week.'

The girls had to stop themselves from groaning aloud at this. But each of them knew that they were being given the extra punishment for the trouble their trick had caused, and they realised that Miss Theobald was being perfectly just.

'That is all,' finished the head, turning her attention to the pile of papers on her desk. 'You may go now.'

Pat, Isabel and Hilary turned towards the door, but Janet remained where she was, looking down at Miss Theobald's bent head. She cleared her throat and said hesitantly, 'Miss Theobald?'

The head looked up sharply. 'What is it, Janet?'

'It . . . it's about Jenny Mills. We're all so sorry that she's been suspended as head girl. What happened that night was nothing to do with her, and –'

'I'm afraid that my decision regarding Jenny must stand,' said the head briskly, though there was a note of regret in her voice. 'The rule about girls remaining in their dormitories at night is a strict one, and there are very good reasons why it must be kept. As head girl, Jenny should have reported the incident and she knows this.'

'But she only acted as she did to keep the second formers from getting into trouble,' protested Pat, turning to face Miss Theobald once more. 'Please, Miss Theobald, couldn't you give her another chance?'

'Not at the moment, I am afraid. I understand Jenny's reasons for not reporting the second formers,' said the head, her tone softening slightly. 'But, as head girl of the whole school it is her duty to stick to the rules. Believe me, Pat, I regret having to suspend her as much as anyone.'

Isabel, who had been frowning thoughtfully, asked suddenly, 'Miss Theobald, how did you know about the second formers being out of their beds that night?'

'Someone took it upon herself to inform me of the

fact,' replied the head, sounding rather scornful. 'And please don't ask me who it was, for even if I knew I would not be able to tell you.'

'Even if you knew?' repeated Hilary, looking puzzled.

'Yes. I am afraid that the person responsible did not have the courage and sense of honour that you girls have shown tonight, but left the information anonymously.'

'You mean that she sent you a letter, Miss Theobald?' said Janet. 'But if that's so, how could you have known that she was telling the truth and not simply making up a story to get Jenny and the second formers into trouble?'

'Because she left me proof,' replied Miss Theobald solemnly. 'Now really, girls, I can't discuss this with you any further. Please return to your common-room now.'

The four girls left, each of them silent until they were out of earshot of the head's room. Then they had plenty to say!

'Miss Theobald said that she couldn't change her mind about Jenny at the moment,' said Isabel, trying hard to look on the bright side. 'Which means that she might at some time in the future. A suspension is only a temporary thing, isn't it?'

'Let's hope so,' said Janet. 'What's puzzling me is what kind of proof the sneak could possibly have given Miss Theobald.'

But none of the others could imagine.

'There's something that doesn't add up about all this,' said Isabel thoughtfully. The others looked at her and she went on, 'We played that trick over a week ago. Why did the sneak wait all this time to go to Miss Theobald?'

'I was wondering that,' said Hilary with a frown. 'It doesn't make any sense at all.'

'I thought of something else, too,' said Janet, looking troubled. 'The sneak has to be a second or third former. No one else knew about the trick.'

'I don't believe for a minute that it's anyone from our form!' cried Isabel, shocked. 'None of them would dream of doing such a sly, underhand thing.'

'What about the new girl, Amanda?' suggested Pat, unable to resist the opportunity to plant doubts in Isabel's mind about her new friend. 'None of us really knows her that well.'

'I do!' protested Isabel, glaring at her twin. 'And I know that she wouldn't dream of doing such a thing! And I notice that you don't mention Kitty. She's new as well, so it could just as easily have been her.'

But no one could really believe that the open, likeable Kitty would be capable of such meanness.

'I suppose it could have been that stepsister of Amanda's – Helen,' said Janet, wrinkling her brow. 'I don't much like her – conceited little beast!'

'I agree, but just because she's conceited that doesn't make her a sneak,' said Hilary. 'Besides, why would she sneak on her own form and get herself into trouble? She couldn't possibly have known that we third formers would own up to Miss Theobald and save their skins.'

'Oh, I don't know! The whole thing's a complete

mystery,' said Janet. 'Anyway, we'd better hurry along to the common-room and tell the others what's happened. I expect they're on tenterhooks.'

Indeed they were! The second and third formers pounced on the four girls as they entered, all of them talking at once.

'What happened, Janet? What did the head say?'

'Yes, tell us what our punishment is.'

'Did Miss Theobald tell you who the sneak is?'

Quickly Janet told them what had happened. There were groans from the third formers when they learned of their punishments, but Grace stood up and said in her clear voice, 'Thank you, Janet – and the rest of you third formers. It was jolly decent of you to take the blame and get us out of trouble.'

'Hear hear!' shouted her form-mates.

'Perhaps now we can put this silly feud behind us,' said Janet, looking at Grace. 'After all, we have more important matters to deal with now.'

Grace nodded and said solemnly, 'I agree. If it wasn't for our quarrel, poor Jenny would still be head girl. I think we should do all we can to get her reinstated.' Her face broke into a grin suddenly. 'I must admit though, Janet, that was a simply splendid trick you played on us – even if it did end up causing so much trouble.'

'Well, at least something good has come out of it,' said Doris happily. 'It will be nice to go to bed tonight without having to check first to see if one of you second formers has put a frog or something in it!'

This was said with such a comical expression that everyone burst out laughing, and suddenly all the ill feeling that had boiled up between the two forms vanished completely.

But there were still very serious matters to discuss, and the laughter soon died when talk returned to the sneak.

'It's horrible to think it might have been one of us,' said Katie, looking round. 'Someone who might be here right now. Ugh!'

'None of us want to think that, Katie,' said Hilary. 'But who else could it have been?'

'Well, who had the most to gain from this?' asked Carlotta, who perched on the edge of a table, swinging her legs.

'What do you mean, Carlotta?' asked Pat, with a frown.

'I mean that maybe we're looking at this from the wrong angle. Perhaps the sneak wasn't out to get us into trouble, but Jenny Mills.'

'Oh, that's impossible!' cried Mirabel. 'Who could have a grudge against old Jenny?'

'No one,' answered Bobby promptly. 'Everyone simply adores her.'

'But there is one person who has got something out of this whole business,' said Carlotta. 'Think about it.'

'Margaret Winters!' cried several girls in unison.

'Of course!' said Pat. 'But how could Margaret do something like that to a member of her own form?'

'I think that Margaret would stop at nothing to get her

own way,' put in the quiet little Gladys. 'And everyone knows that she's always wanted to be head girl.'

'Yes, but how could she possibly have known about the trick we played on the second form?' Isabel asked.

Alison, who had taken no part in this discussion, could have told her cousin exactly how Margaret knew. It was fortunate for her that no one chose to glance in her direction, for Alison's guilty face would certainly have given her away!

'She could have overheard us discussing it,' Kitty was saying now. 'Listening outside doors would be just her style.'

'I suppose so,' said Janet. 'Well, we can't talk about it any more tonight – it's almost bedtime. But I think we should have a meeting in here tomorrow night to plan what we do next.'

Everyone agreed at once, and the girls made their way to bed, all of them in thoughtful mood. But for two girls their thoughts were particularly unhappy, and kept them awake long after the others had gone to sleep.

One was Amanda, whose conscience was troubling her increasingly over what she had done to Pat and Isabel. 'Sly and underhand' – that was what her form had said about the sneak. What would they say about her, Amanda, if they knew how she had intercepted the twins' letters, and that they were hidden away in the locker beside her bed? And how would the twins themselves feel? 'How could she do that to a member of her own form?' That was the question Pat had asked about Margaret Winters, the look of disgust on her face plain to see. Yet what Amanda had done was just as bad – perhaps worse, for she had made her friend unhappy too. Because Isabel was clearly *very* unhappy about the rift that had grown between herself and her twin, no matter how hard she tried to hide it.

And as if that wasn't bad enough, Amanda was also terribly worried about her schoolwork. At her old school she had always been near the top of the class, but the work here was so much more difficult, and no matter how hard she tried she always seemed to be near the bottom. Every week she seemed to fall further behind the others. What if she never caught up, and was kept down next term instead of going up into the fourth with them? It was just too horrible to think about!

The other third former who couldn't sleep was, of course, Alison. No matter how often she told herself that Margaret wasn't the sneak, a niggling little doubt persisted. And if she owned up to the others that she was responsible for letting Margaret in on their secret they would be simply furious with her! Alison didn't think she could bear that. She wouldn't say anything, she decided, until she had seen Margaret tomorrow. Alison was certain that she would be able to tell from the older girl's manner whether she was guilty or not, for surely Margaret wouldn't be able to look her in the face if she had sneaked. Feeling slightly better now that she had made this decision, Alison closed her eyes and tried to get to sleep. Oh dear, what a troublesome term this was turning out to be!

Alison makes a discovery

Alison didn't have long to wait before she encountered Margaret. She was going downstairs to breakfast the very next morning when she heard her name called and, turning, saw the new head girl behind her.

'Alison, I just wanted to say how sorry I was to hear that the third form had got into trouble,' said Margaret, a sympathetic expression on her face. 'Miss Theobald has just told me what happened. What a perfectly horrid ending to such a marvellous trick.' She laid a hand on Alison's shoulder as she spoke, and the girl felt a warm glow spread through her. Margaret sounded so sincere, she couldn't possibly be putting on an act.

'It was rather horrid,' said Alison. 'I just wish we could find out who sneaked.'

'I don't suppose you will, though. I just hope that whoever it was feels thoroughly ashamed of herself,' Margaret said, her eyes sparkling with indignation. 'Oh well, I suppose we'd better go in to breakfast. As head girl I shall be accused of setting a bad example if I'm late. Come and see me after tea, would you, Alison? I've a couple of little jobs for you.'

The girl nodded eagerly before rushing into the big

dining-room to join the rest of her form, feeling more light-hearted than she would have thought possible a short while ago.

The other third formers, however, felt far from light-hearted. Tomorrow was Saturday, and normally they would have been looking forward to going into town to spend their pocket money, or have tea and cakes at the little tea shop. Instead they were to be confined to the school grounds.

Carlotta, who had just opened a letter lying beside her plate, exclaimed, 'Oh, my goodness!'

'What's up, Carlotta?' asked Isabel. 'Not bad news?'

'Far from it, Isabel. My father's just sent me a simply enormous postal order to make up for not being able to visit at half-term. Look!'

'Ooh, you lucky thing!' said Isabel enviously. 'What will you do with all that money?'

'I know what I'd like to do,' replied Carlotta at once, her vivid little face glowing. 'Throw a party!'

'What a marvellous idea,' said Bobby, looking over her shoulder at the postal order. 'My word, Carlotta, I should think you'd be able to feed the whole school with that amount of money!'

Carlotta laughed. 'Well, I wasn't planning on inviting the whole school, Bobby, but it would be nice to ask the second formers, to celebrate the end of our feud.'

There were oohs and aahs at this. 'What a super idea,' said Janet. 'But a party's out of the question until this beastly punishment is over. For one thing we can't go into town to buy the goodies. And for another, Miss Theobald wouldn't allow it while we're in disgrace.'

'No, but there's nothing to stop us planning something for a couple of weeks' time, is there?' said Pat. 'Goodness knows we could do with something to look forward to.'

Everyone agreed to this eagerly and Carlotta said wistfully, 'What a pity we can't hold a midnight feast.'

'Why can't we?' asked Kitty, with a frown. 'Sure, that sounds like a grand idea to me.'

'Kitty, we daren't,' said Hilary. 'It's just too risky. We're already in trouble, and if we're caught I don't like to think what would happen to us.'

'And don't forget that Margaret Winters will be watching us like a hawk,' put in Mirabel, pulling a face. 'She'll just be waiting for a chance to make trouble for us.'

'*More* trouble, you mean,' said Bobby. 'I bet she was absolutely delighted when she found out that Miss Theobald had confined us all to school.'

There were murmurs of agreement at this, but Alison piped up, 'Oh no, you're all wrong! I've just spoken to Margaret, and she told me how sorry she was that we'd all got into trouble.'

'Hmm,' said Janet doubtfully. 'I just bet she was!'

'Honestly, Janet, she was so sincere, and –'

'Oh, Alison!' Isabel interrupted, shaking her head in exasperation. 'You're such a goof that you believe every word Margaret says. And as for her feeling sorry for us – huh!'

Alison's eyes glinted with angry tears, but before a quarrel could erupt Hilary said hastily, 'Kitty, you'd better dash if you're going to give McGinty his breakfast before Geography.'

'So I had,' said the little Irish girl, getting to her feet. 'It's awful grumpy he gets if he's kept waiting for his food.'

'Hold on a minute, Kitty,' said Amanda, rummaging in her satchel. 'I've a couple of apples in here for McGinty. I know how he loves them.'

'Sure, that's awfully kind of you, Amanda. But why don't you come and give them to him yourself?'

Amanda, who was a great animal lover and very fond of McGinty, agreed at once, and the two girls set off together.

The little goat was very pleased to see them, and even more pleased with the bucket of scraps they had brought him.

'You'd think he was starving!' declared Kitty as he polished off the lot.

Amanda laughed and pulled out the brown paper bag containing the apples. But before she had the chance to feed him one, McGinty made a sudden lunge and wolfed down the lot, bag and all.

'Why, I believe he's enjoying the paper more than the apples!' said Amanda, chuckling at the comical appearance McGinty presented, as he stood there with shreds of paper hanging from the corner of his mouth.

'He probably is,' said Kitty, with a grin. 'There's no greater treat than a nice, tasty bit of paper as far as

McGinty's concerned. Come on, boy, just time to take you for a little walk.' She slipped McGinty's lead on and led him to the door. 'Amanda, are you coming?'

Amanda had been staring at the little goat thoughtfully. So, McGinty liked paper, did he? Well, she knew where there was plenty of the stuff, and how to dispose of it was a problem that had been preying on her mind for some time. Maybe McGinty was the answer to her problem. She followed Kitty outside, watching as the goat ate a chocolate wrapper someone had dropped, before nibbling at a patch of grass.

'You know, Miss Theobald really ought to pay me to keep McGinty here,' said Kitty thoughtfully. 'Sure and he earns his keep, getting rid of litter and keeping the grass tidy.'

Amanda opened her mouth to reply, but shut it again quickly, for Margaret Winters was striding towards them, a haughty expression on her face.

'You girls, hurry up!' she commanded briskly. 'Get that animal back where it belongs, or you'll be late for class.'

Looking at Margaret with dislike, Kitty said firmly, 'McGinty is a he, not an it. And if I took him back where he belonged, I would have to travel all the way back to Kilblarney. Then I really would be late!'

Margaret bristled. 'Don't be cheeky, unless you want an order mark. Ugh!' She shuddered and backed away as McGinty raised his head and gently butted his head against her arm. 'I don't know what Miss

Theobald was thinking, to allow such a badly behaved creature at St Clare's!'

Kitty looked up at the head girl, a hurt expression in her blue eyes. 'Ah now, Margaret, that's unkind. Sure and I'm trying so hard to be good!'

Amanda turned her head away, lips clamped tightly together to prevent herself exploding with laughter. Margaret, however, did explode – with anger! At the end of her lecture Kitty was left in no doubt that she was the most insolent, unruly, disrespectful girl ever to darken the doors of St Clare's.

'You'd better be careful, that's all,' Margaret finished, glaring at the younger girl. 'I've got my eye on you – and that goat of yours. If either of you puts a foot wrong –'

'Or a hoof,' broke in the irrepressible Irish girl.

'Kitty,' Amanda said quickly, before a red-faced Margaret could give vent to her fury. 'We really ought to be going, or we shall be awfully late.'

Margaret glanced at her watch and realised that she, too, would be late for class if she didn't hurry. So, contenting herself with a last, angry scowl in Kitty's direction, she stalked off towards the school.

'Kitty, you're dreadful!' said Amanda, as they escorted McGinty safely back to the old stables. 'I wouldn't dare speak to the head girl the way that you do.'

'Ah, as far as I'm concerned, Jenny's still head girl,' answered Kitty, bolting the door firmly behind McGinty. 'And I'm thinking maybe it won't be long before we have her back again!'

Both girls were unusually quiet as they made their way to the Geography lesson, each of them occupied with her own thoughts and schemes. Life at St Clare's was about to get very interesting indeed!

Margaret appeared to be in good humour again when Alison went to her study that evening, behaving so sweetly that the girl was more convinced than ever that she couldn't possibly be the sneak.

'I'm afraid I have to dash off to a meeting now,' said the top former, after she and Alison had drunk their tea. 'Be a dear and clear that pile of books away before you go, would you?'

Alison set to work eagerly once Margaret had gone, picking up the books that had been left on the table and stacking them neatly on a shelf in the cupboard. There was also a cardboard box on the shelf and, as she moved it aside to make room, the lid fell off. Alison saw that the box contained photographs, and couldn't resist taking a peek. There was one of Margaret and her parents, smiling happily at a family party. And another of her with a tall, good-looking young man, who looked so like her that he must be her older brother. Alison sifted happily through the photographs, and was about to put them away when she realised that there were two more in the box, hidden under some negatives. Alison moved the negatives and saw that the last two photographs were different from the others. Margaret and her family weren't on them at all and Alison blinked as she picked them up, hardly able to believe her eyes, then gave a gasp. Hearing a noise in the corridor, she hastily thrust the two photographs and the negatives into her pocket, putting the others back into the cupboard. There was a grim look on her pretty face as she left Margaret's study. She had to speak to the others at once – and it wasn't going to be pleasant!

The common-room was crowded when Alison entered. Girls sat around chattering, one or two reading, some knitting or sewing, while in the corner of the room the radiogram played a lively dance tune.

Alison stood in the doorway for a moment, looking round, before she raised her voice. 'Doris, could you turn the radiogram off, please? There is something I have to tell you all.'

Doris did as she was asked, with a curious glance at Alison. She looked awfully white! Whatever could be wrong?

'What's up, old girl?' asked Isabel, concerned. 'You look terribly pale. Don't say you've fallen out with Margaret!'

Alison's legs suddenly felt dreadfully weak and shaky. She sat down in the nearest armchair and reached into her pocket. 'Take a look at these,' she said, handing the photographs to Janet. 'I found them in Margaret's study.'

The second and third formers crowded curiously round Janet as she looked at the photographs. There was silence for a moment, as they took in what they were seeing.

The first photograph was of the second formers, all in their dressing-gowns, as they huddled together in the grounds, looking furtive. In the middle of them stood Jenny Mills, looking just as guilty as the rest, with her arm round a distressed Katie. The second was even more incriminating, for here Jenny was peering around the corner of the shed, holding a warning hand up to the others. They had obviously been taken on the night of the fateful trick.

'So, this is what Miss Theobald meant by proof,' said Hilary. 'Margaret must have been lying in wait with her camera.'

'I knew that she was the sneak!' said Bobby angrily. 'I just knew it!'

'Good work, Alison!' cried Mirabel.

'Thank goodness we know for certain that no one from the second or third forms was the sneak,' said Grace.

'Yes, but there's just one thing that's puzzling me,' said Janet, who had been looking thoughtful. 'If Margaret was lying in wait, she must have known what we had planned. The question is – who told her?'

Alison swallowed and took a deep breath. Then, in a small voice, she said, 'It was me.'

Amanda is caught out

With many tears from Alison, and much angry prompting
from the others, the whole sorry story unfolded.

'Alison, you're an idiot!' Carlotta told her roundly,
when she had finished. 'Fancy telling Margaret, of all
people, what we were planning. Why, you might just as
well have gone to Miss Theobald herself!'

Alison said nothing, merely sniffed and dabbed at her
eyes. The twins were quite as angry with Alison as
everyone else, but she *was* their cousin, and they tried to
stick up for her.

'Alison didn't *mean* to cause trouble,' said Isabel.

'And Margaret can turn on the charm when she
wants to,' put in Pat. 'I've seen her!'

'Yes, let's not be too hard on Alison,' Kitty added. 'She's
owned up, which can't have been easy. And she's made up
for her mistake by bringing us these photographs.'

'I'll bet Miss Theobald won't be too impressed if we
tell her that the cowardly, anonymous sneak turns out
to be the head girl of St Clare's,' said Isabel. 'It might end
in Margaret being suspended too. You know how Miss
Theobald hates anything underhand.'

'We can't go to the head,' sighed Janet. 'We've no

proof that Margaret took these photographs. It's just our word against hers, and you can bet Margaret will lie her way out of this as she always does.'

'You don't mean that we're just going to let her get away with it?' cried Bobby indignantly.

'It's the last thing in the world I want to do,' Janet said. 'But at the moment, I just can't think of a way to catch her out.'

'This explains why there was such a delay before she snitched on us to the head,' said Grace, who had been looking at the photographs thoughtfully. 'Margaret must have taken the film to the chemist's shop in town to have it developed, and she would have had to wait for the photographs.'

'Alison, you'll have to put them back where you got them from at the earliest opportunity,' said Hilary. 'If Margaret notices that they're missing she'll realise that we're on to her.'

'It's a pity we don't have the negatives,' said Grace, frowning. 'Then I could make a copy of them – just in case dear Margaret takes it into her head to destroy the evidence.'

'But I do have them!' cried Alison, reaching into her pocket once more. 'Is it possible to make a copy from them though?'

'It is if you're a member of the school photography club,' said Grace. 'Which I am. I can slip into the darkroom at break tomorrow morning. There shouldn't be anyone around then.'

'Sure and I'll come with you, Grace,' said Kitty. 'I'm thinking of taking up photography myself.'

The roguish gleam in her eyes made Janet look at her sharply. 'Kitty! You've got something up your sleeve, haven't you?' she said. 'A way of catching Margaret out.'

'Ah now, maybe I have, and maybe I haven't,' Kitty answered, with a teasing smile. 'I don't want to say too much, for I need to think about it and it may not come to anything yet. If my plan is to work, though, I'll be needing accomplices. Alison, you play a very important part.'

Alison, still red-eyed, looked rather alarmed, and the Irish girl went on, 'It's important that Margaret doesn't suspect anything, so you must carry on doing her jobs, and being just as friendly towards her as you've always been. Can you do that?'

'Oh, Kitty, I don't think I can!' said Alison dolefully. 'I feel so betrayed and let down that I really don't think I can even look at her again.'

'Don't be such a goof, Alison!' said Janet sharply. 'You got us all into this mess – the least you can do is help us to get out of it.'

'Janet's right,' said Pat. 'You owe it to all of us to try and put things right.'

'Yes, come on, Alison!' Doris cried bracingly. 'This is your chance to be a heroine.'

This instantly appealed to Alison's sense of the dramatic, and the thought of getting back into the others' good books cheered her enormously. 'Very well,' she said, squaring her slim shoulders. 'It won't be easy being pleasant to Margaret but, for the sake of our two forms, I shall sacrifice my pride.'

One or two of the girls had to turn away to hide their smiles at this, but Kitty said, 'That's the spirit, Alison! And there's something else that I want the rest of you to do.'

'Anything, Kitty,' said Bobby promptly. 'If it's going to help us show Margaret Winters up for the sly, deceitful creature she is, I'm all for it!'

'Good. Because I want you all to go ahead and organise that midnight feast we were talking about earlier. Goodness knows we need something to cheer us up a bit!'

There was silence as the second and third formers looked at one another in amazement. This was the last thing they had expected Kitty to ask of them.

At last Hilary spoke. 'Kitty, are you quite mad? As I explained this morning, it's just too dangerous. If Margaret starts snooping round . . .'

'Ah now, don't you go worrying your head about Margaret,' said Kitty soothingly. 'She'll not be doing any snooping, I promise you. Not if my little scheme comes off.'

The girls were in two minds. On the one hand, they certainly didn't want to get into any more trouble. But on the other hand, a midnight feast would be too wizard for words! As always, they looked to their head girls for a lead.

'I vote we do as Kitty says,' said Grace firmly. 'Janet?'

Janet looked at the Irish girl thoughtfully for a moment, her head on one side. 'I trust you, Kitty,' she said at last. 'Though I don't know why, for you do the craziest things! A feast it is, then – but just make sure you don't let us down.'

'That was a very brave thing you did earlier,' said Amanda, coming up to Alison in the dormitory that evening. 'It must have been difficult, owning up to what you had done in front of everyone like that.'

'I don't feel as if I'm a very brave person,' said Alison honestly. 'But once I'd discovered those photographs I really didn't have much choice in the matter. I do feel better for it, though – as if a great weight has been lifted from my shoulders.'

Amanda could understand that, for she, too, had been carrying a great weight around with her for quite a while, and it seemed to get a little heavier each day. She looked at Alison's pretty, kindly face and, for a moment, thought about confiding in the girl. Alison might be silly at times, but she was kind-hearted and sensitive to the feelings of others. But she was also the twins' cousin, a little voice in Amanda's head reminded her. It was highly probable that Alison's loyalty to Pat and Isabel would make her run straight to them and blurt out her, Amanda's, secret. No, she could not risk letting Alison know what troubled her.

But Amanda would have to find some way of easing her conscience, which was beginning to cause her sleepless nights. And then she was tired and stupid in class, and got even further behind with her work, which made her worry about that as well! Perhaps getting rid of those wretched letters would ease the burden a little. It wouldn't change what she had done, but at least they wouldn't be there in her locker, right beside her as she tried to sleep, a constant reminder of her deceit and wickedness. Yes, tomorrow – with McGinty's help – she would dispose of them.

'Well, this is no way to spend a Saturday afternoon,' grumbled Bobby the next day, as the third form sat rather listlessly in the common-room. Even the luxury of having it all to themselves didn't cheer them, when they thought of the second formers happily shopping and having their tea in town. And the fact that they only had themselves to blame for their confinement didn't make the punishment any easier to bear.

'It's the first fine day we've had all week, too,' sighed Carlotta, looking wistfully out of the window.

'Well, why don't we go outside?' suggested Hilary, brightening suddenly. 'Miss Theobald said we weren't allowed outside the grounds, but there's no reason why we have to stay cooped up indoors.'

'Good idea,' said Janet. 'Let's get our coats and go for a walk round the gardens.'

The others leaped to their feet eagerly, only Amanda remaining in her seat.

'Come on, Amanda!' cried Isabel. 'Let's get some fresh air.'

'Actually, Isabel, I think I'll just stay here and finish my book,' said the girl. 'I've got a bit of a cold coming on.'

'I thought you'd been looking a bit peaky lately,' Isabel said. 'Would you like me to stay and keep you company?'

'Thanks, Isabel, but I'll be fine,' said Amanda, smiling wanly. 'You go off with the others and enjoy yourself.'

So Isabel left and, after a few moments, Amanda went to the window. She could see the third formers heading towards the playing fields and breathed a sigh of relief. The coast was clear.

Running up to the dormitory, Amanda pulled on her hat and coat, before taking the twins' letters from her locker. The girl shuddered as she stuffed them into her satchel. Just a few sheets of paper – but what a lot of trouble they had stirred up!

In a few minutes Amanda had reached the old stables. Looking around furtively to make sure no one was about, she slipped inside and received a warm welcome from McGinty.

'Are you hungry, boy?' she whispered. 'Well, not for much longer. I have a special treat for you.'

With that, Amanda pulled a couple of the letters from her satchel, McGinty snatching them from her and making short work of them. Amanda fed him another, then another, so intent on what she was doing that she didn't even notice one of the envelopes fall from her bag and on to the floor. Nor did she hear the door open softly behind her.

'Nearly finished now, McGinty,' murmured Amanda. 'Have you room for one more?'

Again she reached into her satchel, giving a gasp when she found it empty. Amanda was certain that there had been one more letter! Suppose she had dropped it in the grounds on the way here? Worse still, what if it was lying on the floor in the dormitory, where anyone could find it? A shiver went down her spine. She had to retrace her steps at once and find that letter. Quickly Amanda turned – and came face to face with Janet!

'Looking for this, Amanda?' said Janet coolly, holding out her hand. In it was the missing letter.

Amanda turned white, but tried to bluff it out. 'Wh – what's that?' she asked, her voice sounding unnaturally high with nerves.

'You know what it is!' Janet said scornfully. 'So don't try to act all innocent with me. I know what you've been up to, Amanda, and I saw you feeding the twins' letters to McGinty, so you may as well do the decent thing and own up.'

At once Amanda saw that there was no point in lying. She had been caught red-handed!

14

A very unhappy girl

As Janet stood watching her, arms folded and a stern expression on her face, the only thing Amanda could think of to say was, 'I thought you had gone for a walk with the others.'

'That was what you were supposed to think,' Janet said. 'Actually I told them that I'd changed my mind and decided to stay behind with you. Then I hid round the corner by the common-room and waited to see if my suspicions were correct. I had a feeling you'd want to get rid of those letters pretty soon.'

All at once Amanda's legs seemed to turn to jelly, and she sat down on a rickety old chair that had been dumped in the stables. 'But how did you know?' she whispered, staring at Janet in bewilderment. 'What made you suspect me?'

'Actually, it was something Carlotta said,' Janet told her. 'The day Jenny Mills was suspended. "Who had the most to gain?" she asked. Do you remember?'

Horrified, Amanda nodded.

'That got me thinking,' Janet went on. 'And I asked myself who had the most to gain from ensuring that the twins didn't receive their letters to one another. The answer was you, Amanda. I began to watch you, and noticed how nervous and unhappy you seemed – and how uncomfortable you looked whenever anyone brought the subject of those letters up. That's when I knew that I was right.'

'Janet, please don't tell Pat and Isabel,' begged Amanda. 'I would lose Isabel's friendship and I couldn't bear that.'

'That's why you did it, isn't it?' said Janet. 'You were afraid that, once Pat came back, Isabel wouldn't want you around any more.'

Miserably Amanda nodded. 'It was terribly wrong of me, I know, but, you see, I've never really had a friend of my own before.'

'Haven't you?' said Janet, surprised and a little disbelieving. Surely everyone had friends! 'Why ever not?'

'Well, when it was just Mummy and I, we lived in a little cottage in a remote village. I went to day school in the nearest town, which was where most of the other girls lived. But because our cottage was such a long way out, I could never invite anyone home to tea, or go to their birthday parties. Soon people became fed up with me refusing their invitations all the time and just left me alone. I think they thought I was a bit stuck-up and didn't want to make friends when, actually, I was desperately lonely. I would have given anything for someone to laugh and joke with, and share secrets with.'

'Golly, how awful!' said Janet, beginning to feel a

little sorry for Amanda. 'But why didn't you try to make friends with Helen when your parents got married? Surely that would have been a perfect solution.'

Amanda laughed bitterly. 'I was so thrilled when Mummy announced that she and Helen's father were getting married and that I was to have a stepsister. I tried so hard to be her friend, and to make her like me. But Helen never gave me a chance. She looked down her nose at me from the start, and made it very plain that we were never going to be friends.'

It just went to show, thought Janet, that things were never quite as they seemed. She had come in here prepared to tear Amanda off a strip, before hauling her in front of the third form so that they could decide on a punishment. Now, though, although what Amanda had done was very wrong, Janet felt that the girl needed helping rather than punishing. At last she said, 'It seems to me, Amanda, that you have done a bad thing for a good reason. But Pat and Isabel have to be told. It's only fair.'

Amanda nodded unhappily and said, 'Will you have to tell all the others as well?'

'That will be for the twins to decide,' answered Janet, moving towards the door. 'Wait here and I'll go and find them.'

'You're going to bring them here now?' squeaked Amanda, in alarm.

Janet nodded. 'I think you should own up to them yourself, Amanda – and the sooner the better. Just be honest, and tell them exactly what you have told me. They're both fair and decent, and although they will probably be angry at first, I don't think that they will be too hard on you.'

Then she was gone, leaving poor Amanda alone with her own thoughts. They were not pleasant ones, and the next few minutes seemed to pass very slowly indeed. At last Janet returned with the twins, Isabel looking puzzled, and Pat looking displeased at having her walk interrupted.

'Janet said that you wanted to speak to us,' said Isabel. 'What's up, old girl?'

The concern in her voice made Amanda feel guiltier than ever. She glanced at Janet, who nodded encouragingly. So, taking a deep breath, she began. The twins were silent for a few moments when they learned that it was Amanda who had caused the rift between them. Isabel found her voice first. She was so shocked to learn of her friend's deceit that she had scarcely taken in the other things Amanda had admitted to – her feelings of loneliness, and her fear of losing her first true friend.

'How could you, Amanda?' she cried, two angry spots of colour on her cheeks. 'I trusted you and thought we were friends. But you're no friend of mine.'

This was exactly what Amanda had feared, and she began to sob, burying her face in her hands. Someone moved across to her, placing a comforting arm about her shoulders, and Amanda lifted her head, giving a shocked gasp when she saw who it was. Pat! But why? Amanda knew how bitterly Isabel's twin resented her, for she had not attempted to hide her hostility. Yet here she was offering her comfort! Amanda could not understand it. Nor could Isabel, who cried, 'Pat, how can you feel sorry for her after what she's done to us?'

'Because, believe it or not, I can understand *why* she did it,' said Pat, keeping her arm around the weeping Amanda. 'You and I have been lucky, Isabel. We've always had one another, as well as our friends here at St Clare's. But Amanda didn't have a friend in the world until she met you.'

Isabel's brow puckered thoughtfully and Pat went on, 'I can sympathise with her, because, for the past few weeks, I've felt that I was in danger of losing you too.'

'Oh, Pat,' said Isabel, tears starting to her eyes. 'You'll never lose me! No matter what happens, you and I will *always* have one another.'

Janet, who had remained in the background petting McGinty, joined the other three now, and said in her forthright way, 'Well, you don't know how glad I am to hear that!'

The twins laughed, rather shakily, and Pat said, 'But what are we going to do about Amanda?'

'I was rather wondering that myself,' came Amanda's plaintive voice, as she pulled a handkerchief from her pocket and dabbed at her eyes.

'I don't think we should tell the others,' said Pat firmly. 'That would only turn them against Amanda, which would make matters worse.'

'I agree,' said Isabel. 'We'll just tell them that we've sorted out the mix-up over the letters and that everything is all right between us now.'

'Do you mean that?' gasped Amanda, beginning to look more hopeful. 'It's more than I deserve after I played such a mean trick on you both.'

'It *was* a mean trick,' said Isabel gravely. 'But everyone deserves a second chance.'

'Come on, Amanda,' said Janet, taking the girl's arm and pulling her to her feet. 'You'd better wash your face, or the others will start asking questions if they see you with red eyes at the tea-table. And I rather think that the twins have things to talk about.'

'We do,' said Isabel, as Janet led Amanda away.

But, as she reached the door, Amanda turned and said, 'Isabel! Are we still . . .'

'Yes, we're still friends,' said Isabel. 'Pat?'

'I'd like to be friends with you too, Amanda,' Pat said with a smile. 'You see, that's the thing with twins – if you're friends with one, you have to be friends with the other too. I hope you don't mind.'

'Mind?' repeated Amanda incredulously. 'Why, I'm thrilled. Having both of you as my friends will be too marvellous for words!'

'Thank heavens for that!' laughed Janet. 'Now Amanda and I are going indoors, and you two had better not be far behind unless you want to be late for tea.'

As the door closed behind the two girls there was silence for a moment then, at the same time, both Pat and Isabel cried, 'Let's never quarrel again!'

They laughed and Pat said, 'I'm sorry I doubted you, old thing.'

'And I'm sorry too,' said Isabel. 'I should have known that you wouldn't have suddenly stopped writing to me for no reason.'

'I'm so glad we're friends again,' said Pat happily, slipping her arm through Isabel's. 'I just wish there was something we could do to help Amanda.'

'So do I,' sighed Isabel. 'If only she and Helen could settle their differences I really think that the pair of them would be much happier.'

'Yes, we must put our thinking caps on and see if there's something we can do to bring the two of them together.'

But, as things turned out, Pat and Isabel didn't need to put their thinking caps on at all!

In the common-room that evening Helen was in an extremely bad temper, having been given several stockings to darn by Matron. 'I hate darning,' she complained, for about the twentieth time, and Grace rolled her eyes.

'If you concentrate on what you're doing, instead of moaning about it, you'll get it done much more quickly,' she said sensibly.

'Katie, can't you help me?' pleaded Helen. 'You're good at needlework.'

'No,' Katie said bluntly. 'I've finished my own

mending and I've no intention of doing yours as well.'

Helen's expression was so sulky that Amanda, sitting nearby, laughed. The second former glared at her, then said, 'Of course, if I was at home I would simply throw these old stockings away and get Daddy to buy me new ones. Amanda, perhaps you could give me a hand. After all, you're used to having to mend things and go on wearing them when they're worn out and shabby.'

'That's enough!' said Grace sharply. But it was too late.

Amanda laughed and said, 'Do you know, Helen, I often wonder how someone as kind and sweet-natured as your father came to have a daughter like you. I really feel sorry for him at times.'

'Well, I feel sorry for your mother,' retorted Helen angrily. 'Being poor *and* having to live in a tiny cottage with only *you* for company must have been simply dreadful. Thank heavens Daddy came along and rescued her.'

'Here we go again,' muttered Janet under her breath, as the quarrel grew more heated. She and Grace exchanged glances, and were just about to step in and break things up when Gladys suddenly got to her feet and shouted, 'Will you two SHUT UP!'

The stepsisters were so astonished at being yelled at by the timid little third former that they did just that!

'The two of you ought to be ashamed of yourselves,' Gladys went on, looking angrier than the girls had ever seen her. 'You are both so lucky to have two parents to love you and take care of you, but you're so intent on rowing with one another that you don't appreciate it at all! Why, if my mother met a nice man who could be like a father to me, and if I had a sister or brother to share my happiness with, I would think myself the luckiest girl in the world!'

Everyone knew that Gladys's father had died when she was small, and that her mother had struggled to bring her up alone. Remembering this, Amanda turned red, and even Helen looked shame-faced.

'Gladys is perfectly right,' said Carlotta, going across and giving the girl a pat on the shoulder. 'I only have a father, because my mother died when I was a baby, and I feel just as Gladys does. You two should learn to count your blessings. And if you can't manage to do that, save your quarrels for when you're alone and stop making everyone else feel uncomfortable!' She glared fiercely at the two girls, who didn't dare resume their quarrel after that.

Helen finished her darning in silence, while Amanda buried her head in a book. But everyone noticed that, when bedtime came, they managed to say goodnight to one another in quite a civil manner.

'Good old Gladys,' murmured Pat to Isabel. 'Let's hope that this is a new beginning for Amanda and Helen.'

It was. At breakfast the next morning, Amanda opened a letter from her mother, and gave a gasp as she read it. 'Oh my goodness! I don't believe it!'

'Don't believe what?' asked Doris, looking quite alarmed.

'It's my mother,' said Amanda. 'And Helen's father. They're going to have a baby. I'm going to be a sister!'

Pat looked up sharply, curious to know how Amanda felt about the news. One look at the girl's face left her in no doubt – Amanda was beaming from ear to ear! As the third formers called out their congratulations, Helen, at the second-form table, let out a cry and it was obvious that she, too, had received the news.

'Amanda!' she called, standing up and waving the letter in the air. 'Have you heard?'

'Yes, isn't it simply marvellous?' Amanda called back.

'I'll say,' laughed Helen, whose genuinely happy smile made her look really pretty. 'The most thrilling news ever.'

Mam'zelle, who was at the mistresses' table, stood up and called both girls to order.

'Sorry, Mam'zelle,' said Amanda, unable to stop grinning. 'But, you see, we've just learned that our parents – Helen's and mine – are expecting a baby!'

'Ah, that is indeed good news!' cried Mam'zelle, clapping her hands together and smiling. 'A dear little *bébé*. Amanda, you may take your meal over to the second-form table. You and Helen will wish to talk about your new brother or sister.'

Amanda picked up her plate at once, while Helen moved up to make room for her. The others looked on in amusement.

'I do hope it's a boy,' said Helen, as Amanda sat down. 'It would be such fun to have a little brother.'

'Yes, though a girl would be nice too,' Amanda said. 'Or twins – one of each!'

'Well!' said Isabel, with a laugh. 'It looks as though this new baby has done the trick.'

'You don't mind, do you?' said Pat. 'Amanda going off with Helen, I mean.'

'Not a bit,' said Isabel happily. 'I'm just glad that the two of them finally seem to be getting on. And, to be honest, it will be nice to have you to myself for a bit.'

Pat grinned and said, 'When breakfast's over let's find a quiet corner and go and have a good old chat before lessons start. Just the two of us.'

'Yes,' said Isabel. 'Won't that be nice? Just the two of us.'

Kitty's secret plan

The third form's two weeks of punishment were up, and plans for the midnight feast were in full swing.

'We'd better hold it in here,' said Janet, looking round the common-room one evening. 'Neither of the dorms is big enough.'

'And we can use the big cupboard over there to store all the goodies,' said Bobby, rubbing her hands together. 'Whoopee, I can't wait! When's it to be?'

'How about next Saturday?' suggested Hilary.

Kitty, who had been looking at the calendar on the wall, turned and said, 'Sure, Friday would be better.'

'Oh? Why's that, Kitty?' asked Mirabel.

'There will be a full moon, for one thing,' answered Kitty.

'What difference does that make?' Doris asked, puzzled. 'We shall all be indoors anyway.'

'*You* will be,' said Kitty. 'But I'll be spending part of the evening outside and it'll be good to have some light. Alison, do you think I could have a word with you?'

'Of course,' said Alison, getting up and following the Irish girl into the corridor.

Kitty looked up and down then, satisfied they could

not be overheard, said, 'Did you know, Alison, that some people believe the full moon causes madness in animals?'

'Er, no, Kitty, I didn't know that,' said Alison, frowning. 'It's very interesting, but surely you didn't bring me out here to tell me that?'

'I did. For I want you to make sure Margaret knows that McGinty is prone to moon madness,' said Kitty with a grin. 'Tell her that it's awful worried I am that he might escape from his stable and go on the rampage on the night of the full moon.'

Alison nodded, her eyes wide, and Kitty went on, 'Then I want you to tell her that he's been misbehaving dreadfully, and that Miss Theobald has told me he's on his last chance at St Clare's. If he gets into one more scrape he's to be sent away. Now, have you got all that, Alison?'

'Yes, but *why* do you want me to tell Margaret all this?' asked Alison.

'Ah, never you mind,' said Kitty. 'You and all the others will find out soon enough. Now, I must go and speak to Grace.'

Kitty had been spending quite a lot of time with Grace lately, learning all she could from her about photography. The others knew that this had something to do with Kitty's great plan, and were simply bursting with curiosity. But Kitty, enjoying herself enormously, would tell them nothing, merely saying infuriatingly, 'All in good time!'

Gradually the big cupboard in the common-room began to fill up, as preparations for the feast went ahead. The twins opened the door one day to put away a tin of biscuits they had bought, and Isabel's eyes lit up as she saw all the good things piled up there.

'Tins of pineapple, prawns and sardines – yummy! And just look at this simply enormous box of chocolates! My word, what a feast this is going to be.'

'I'll say,' said Pat. 'And that big iced cake looks simply gorgeous. I wonder who bought that?'

'Amanda and Helen bought it between them,' said Isabel. 'Who would have thought that they would become so close all of a sudden – and all thanks to a baby!'

'Well, this baby will be brother or sister to both of them,' said Pat. 'So at last they will have something they can share.'

'And a jolly good thing too,' said Isabel. Then she gave a laugh. 'I wonder how long it will be before the two of them are arguing over whose turn it is to babysit!'

But, for the moment, the stepsisters were the best of friends, and seemed to have put their differences behind them. Helen's happiness seemed to have made her forget her snobbish ways and, as a result, she was much more popular with her form too. In fact, the whole of the second form and the whole of the third form were getting on together very well indeed. So much so that, when Miss Theobald came into the common-room that evening, to make what she thought would be a happy announcement, there was consternation.

Everyone rose to their feet when the head entered, and Helen immediately turned off the gramophone.

'Sit down, girls,' said Miss Theobald, smiling round. 'I shan't take up much of your evening. I have just come to tell you that work on the second form's quarters is finished. I know it has taken a little longer than we expected but, for the last week of term, you third formers will have your common-room to yourselves again. The new dormitory has yet to be painted, so I'm afraid your sleeping arrangements will remain as they are for the rest of the term.'

'Thank you, Miss Theobald,' said the two head girls, in rather a subdued manner. It was funny, but after all the complaints about being cramped, and having no privacy and, of course, the big feud, each form now realised that it was going to miss the other.

Miss Theobald, who had expected cheers, was most surprised at the way the girls received the news. But, after being head of St Clare's for many years, she had learned that girls often behaved unexpectedly!

'Amanda, my dear,' she said. 'I wonder if you could come to my room for a few moments. There is something I need to discuss with you.'

'Yes, Miss Theobald,' said the girl politely, feeling surprised and rather nervous. Whatever could the head want to speak to her about?

'Well,' said Janet, flopping down into an armchair, after Miss Theobald and Amanda had left. 'It's going to be jolly quiet in here without you second formers.'

'I thought you couldn't wait to get rid of us,' said Grace, with a grin.

'So did I,' said Janet, with her usual honesty. 'But now that it's almost time for you to leave, I'm not so sure I like the idea.'

'I daresay you'll soon get used to being without us,' said Grace. 'It is going to be strange for a while though. You third formers aren't really such a bad lot, you know.'

'Thanks,' said Janet, with a smile. 'I say, I wonder what Miss Theobald wants with Amanda?'

'I was wondering that too,' said Helen, frowning. 'I do hope she's not in any trouble.'

But Amanda wasn't in trouble, although what Miss Theobald had to say was very important. She wasted no time in getting straight to the point. 'Miss Adams has been speaking to me about you, Amanda, and she is a little concerned that you are finding the work of the third form too difficult. This is no reflection on you, as she tells me that you are an extremely hard worker and always try your best. However, as you are a little younger than most of the third, it is perhaps not surprising that you have found it hard to keep up with them. You really should have been in the second form from the start, but your mother felt that you might settle in better away from your stepsister. I understand that the two of you don't get on?'

'We *didn't* get on,' admitted Amanda. 'But that's all been sorted out now. Helen and I realised how silly we had been and have made friends now.'

'That is very good news,' said Miss Theobald with her charming smile. 'And it makes it very much easier to tell you why I have asked you here. You see, my dear, Miss Adams feels that you aren't ready to join the fourth form with the others next term – and I agree with her. So, we have decided that it is for the best if you remain in the third form, along with the second formers, who will be going up after the holidays. How do you feel about that?'

'It's funny,' said Amanda, wrinkling her brow. 'I always dreaded that this would happen, and now that it has – I don't actually mind. I shall miss being with Pat and Isabel and the rest, but I'm quite looking forward to spending more time with Helen. Though I expect we will still argue from time to time.'

'I expect that you will,' laughed Miss Theobald. 'I believe that all sisters do. I am very pleased with your sensible attitude to this, Amanda. Now you may go and join the others.'

'There you are!' said Isabel, when Amanda returned to the common-room. 'What did Miss Theobald want?'

Amanda told her, the others gathering round to listen.

'What a shame!' cried Hilary. 'It would have been sport if you could have come up into the fourth with us.'

'Well, your loss is our gain,' said Grace, clapping Amanda on the shoulder. 'I know it's a bit early, as you won't actually be joining us until after the hols, but welcome to our form.'

'Golly, what a good thing we aren't feuding any

more,' said Harriet. 'You wouldn't know whose side to be on, Amanda.'

Everyone laughed, and the twins came up on either side of Amanda, each of them taking one of her arms.

'She's still a member of our form, for now,' said Pat grinning. 'Come and help Isabel and me with this jigsaw, and never mind these kids.'

Amanda smiled too, feeling a warm glow inside. How lovely it felt to be wanted! And she had so much to look forward to, as well – a new brother or sister, the holidays – and, of course, the midnight feast!

Part of Kitty's plan seemed to be to annoy Margaret, which she did most effectively and at every opportunity. Whenever the head girl appeared, Kitty would start running in the corridor, or yelling loudly, earning herself a stern ticking off. The final straw, for Margaret, came two days before the feast was to take place, when Kitty arrived in the dining-room ten minutes after the bell had gone for tea.

'Kitty Flaherty!' thundered Margaret, as the Irish girl sauntered in. 'This is the third time this week you've been late for tea. Report to my study at six o'clock.'

'Yes, Margaret,' said Kitty meekly, her laughing eyes downcast.

'I bet she'll give you lines,' said Carlotta, as Kitty took her place at the table.

'Sure and I'm not bothered about that,' Kitty said, helping herself to a sandwich. 'It's all going to be worth it in the end, Carlotta. You'll see.'

Margaret was poring over her maths prep when Kitty reported to her, and she stared at the girl coldly. 'Well?' she snapped. 'What have you got to say for yourself?'

'I'm sorry I was late, Margaret,' said Kitty politely. 'But it took me longer than usual to settle McGinty. He's become awful restless lately, because –'

'I'm not the slightest bit interested in that animal,' Margaret interrupted. 'I want you to write me a five-hundred-word essay on punctuality, and hand it in to me on Sunday.'

'Very well, Margaret,' said Kitty, sighing heavily. Then she frowned. 'Ah, there's a fly just landed on your maths book there! Let me swat it for you.' And, flapping her hands wildly, Kitty leaned over the desk – knocking Margaret's ink bottle all over her neatly written prep!

'You idiot!' shrieked Margaret, jumping to her feet before the ink could drip on to her skirt.

'Oh, Margaret, I'm so sorry!' exclaimed Kitty, putting her hand up to her mouth in horror. 'Ah, it's awful clumsy I am!'

'Clumsy? I believe you did it on purpose!' cried the head girl, quite beside herself with rage. 'I spent hours on that prep, and now I shall have to do it all again.'

'Let me clean it up,' said Kitty contritely. 'Ah, this old cloth will do the job!'

Before Margaret could stop her, the Irish girl snatched up a piece of cloth that was hanging over the back of a chair and began mopping up the spilled ink with it.

'Stop!' yelled Margaret. 'That old cloth happens to be my best scarf!'

'Oh no!' wailed Kitty, dropping the scarf instantly and clutching at Margaret's arm. 'Now what's to be done?'

'Get off me, you stupid girl,' Margaret hissed, brushing Kitty's inky hand away. 'You're getting ink stains all over my sleeve now. Oh, just get out before you do any more damage!'

Lowering her head to hide a grin, Kitty said in a very subdued tone, 'I really am sorry, Margaret.'

'Oh, don't put on that meek and mild act with me!' snapped Margaret. 'I know that what you did was deliberate, and I'll get back at you somehow, Kitty Flaherty!'

This was just what Kitty wanted to hear, and she hummed to herself as she washed the ink from her hands before joining her friends. Margaret would well and truly have it in for her now – and that was going to be her downfall!

Alison played her part the following evening. Margaret couldn't wait to pour out the story of Kitty's dreadful behaviour, and Alison listened open-mouthed. 'Well!' she said at last, when Margaret had finished. 'I thought Kitty looked pleased with herself last night, and now I know why.'

Margaret gasped. 'That just proves that the little beast did it on purpose. I honestly don't think she cares tuppence for anyone's opinion!'

'She doesn't,' said Alison, with a sniff. 'I think all she

cares about is that horrible goat of hers. Of course, she's awfully worried about him at the moment. He's been in a few scrapes lately, and Miss Theobald has warned Kitty that if he causes any more trouble, she will have to send him away from St Clare's.'

'Really?' said Margaret, her eyes narrowing keenly.

'And, of course, Kitty's got this silly idea that he's going to go mad tomorrow night, because of the full moon,' Alison went on.

'Full moon?' repeated Margaret, baffled.

Alison nodded. 'Apparently some animals go completely potty when there's a full moon – and McGinty is one of them. Kitty says he becomes completely uncontrollable, and she's terrified that he'll escape from the stables and run wild.'

'And if he does, he's for the high jump,' murmured Margaret.

'That's right,' said Alison. 'And so is Kitty.'

Margaret seemed distracted after that, and soon found an excuse to get rid of Alison. She needed to be alone, to think and to scheme. That Irish girl had gone too far this time, and now she was going to pay for it.

Alison, for her part, was extremely pleased with the way she had duped Margaret. Really, she ought to be an actress, for the head girl had believed every word she said. Alison felt quite smug when she went to find Kitty, saying triumphantly, 'She fell for it, hook, line and sinker. And I'm betting she means to make things pretty hot for you and McGinty.'

'Let her try,' said Kitty with a grin. 'I'm afraid our dear head girl is about to find out that she's bitten off more than she can chew!'

Alison laughed. 'I don't know what I'm more excited about, Kitty – our feast, or your revenge on Margaret. Oh, I can't wait for tomorrow night!'

16

Midnight fun

The second and third formers were in a state of great excitement the following day, and not in the mood to concentrate on their lessons at all. Miss Jenks grew so exasperated with her form that she threatened to set them an extra hour's prep that evening. This made them sit up and pay attention at once, as their plans for that evening most definitely did not include extra prep!

Pat, Isabel and Amanda whispered together almost continuously through their English lesson, and Miss Adams became extremely annoyed. 'If I hear one more whisper, or one more giggle, from you three girls, I shall send you all out of the room,' she snapped.

'Sorry, Miss Adams,' chorused the three, trying their best to look serious.

'So you should be,' said the mistress crisply. 'Now, instead of talking among yourselves, please listen to what I have to say and you might actually learn something!'

But not even Miss Adams' short temper could dampen the girls' high spirits as they waited eagerly for bedtime.

At last it arrived, and the girls trooped upstairs.

Janet said, 'Grace, don't forget to set your alarm

clock. It would be simply awful if you all slept through the feast.'

'No chance of that, Janet,' laughed Grace. 'We'll be there all right. Now, come along, everyone. Let's try and get some sleep.'

Janet and Grace were to be responsible for waking everyone – all except Kitty, who slipped out of bed an hour before everyone else and put on her coat and outdoor shoes. She had no idea what time Margaret would show up, and didn't want to risk missing her. That would ruin everything!

'Kitty?' whispered Bobby, who was still awake. 'Is that you?'

'Yes, I've something important to do,' Kitty whispered back. 'Now don't worry if I'm not back in time for the start of the feast, Bobby. But save me some food, for I'll be hungry.'

'All right. Take care, Kitty.'

And, with a wave, the girl slipped from the room, ran down the stairs and out into the night.

At midnight the others awoke, making their way quickly and quietly to the common-room. Carlotta and Doris lit candles and placed them around the room. Hilary, Mirabel and Gladys pushed the furniture back against the walls to make more space. And the others got the food from the store cupboard and began setting it out.

'This looks delicious!' said Katie, when everything was ready.

'I should say,' agreed Harriet. 'Jolly decent of you third formers to invite us to share.'

'Hear, hear!' chorused the rest of the second form, all of them raising tooth mugs of ginger beer to the third form.

'Tuck in, everyone,' said Janet, sitting on the floor and opening an enormous tin of pineapple. 'Don't forget to save a little bit of everything for Kitty, though.'

'We won't,' said Bobby. 'I wonder what she's doing now?'

Kitty was, in fact, hidden in an empty stall in the old stables. It was a chilly night and, despite a thick coat, scarf and gloves, she felt extremely cold. She felt stiff, too, from sitting in the same position for so long, and thought enviously of the others enjoying their feast. But despite the cold and discomfort, Kitty was determined to stay where she was, absolutely certain that Margaret would take the bait and walk right into her trap. Kitty just hoped she wouldn't have to wait too much longer.

Five minutes later her patience was rewarded. A beam of torchlight played on the floor as a shadowy figure appeared. Kitty held her breath, sure that the intruder must be able to hear her heart pounding. The figure advanced into the stables and Kitty was able to see quite clearly who it was. Margaret!

McGinty made a bleating sound as the head girl approached and she hushed him, getting his lead down from the wall and slipping it round his neck.

'You're coming with me,' she said, producing a carrot

from the bag she carried and dangling it in front of him. 'Hurry up!'

The carrot did the trick and McGinty trotted along beside Margaret, trying to snatch the treat from her hand. Eventually he succeeded and, once he had eaten it, refused to budge another inch until she had produced more food. It soon became apparent that she was heading for the little kitchen garden, and Kitty followed, moving stealthily under cover of the trees and bushes. The short walk took some time, as McGinty's demands for food were frequent, but at last Margaret reached her destination. She removed McGinty's lead and opened the little gate, saying under her breath, 'Go on then, you greedy creature – help yourself.'

The garden was full of herbs and vegetables and, normally, McGinty would have been in seventh heaven. Now, however, he moved slowly through the gate and sat down.

'What's the matter with you?' Margaret hissed, prodding him with the toe of her shoe. 'Get up!'

But, alas for Margaret, she had fed the goat so well that he simply wasn't interested in the contents of the kitchen garden. All he wanted to do was sit quietly for a while and let his unexpected supper go down. Kitty grinned to herself in the darkness. Oh dear! What was Margaret going to do now?

For a moment the head girl seemed at a loss, then her lips tightened determinedly and she stepped through the gate, muttering, 'Well, I'll just have to do the job myself. You and your mistress will still get the blame, which is all that matters!'

And, under Kitty's astonished, horrified gaze, Margaret began to destroy the little garden. Plants were trampled, broken, uprooted and scattered everywhere, the head girl so intent on making trouble for Kitty that she cared nothing for the destruction she caused. The expression of spite on her face made Kitty shiver.

At last, panting from her exertion, Margaret stood back and leaned on the fence, a triumphant smile on her face as she shone her torch beam over the ruined garden. Now all that remained was for her to shut the gate so that McGinty couldn't get out. Tomorrow he would be discovered – and banished from St Clare's. And no one would ever dream of suspecting that the head girl had had anything to do with it. Even Kitty would assume that the goat's 'moon madness' had got the better of him. Margaret yawned, feeling quite worn out. Longing for her bed, she turned to go through the gate. But the torch slipped from her fingers and, with an exclamation of annoyance, she bent to pick it up. McGinty, who was beginning to feel a little more lively, got up and watched her. Despite the fact that she had fed him well, McGinty didn't care for Margaret. He didn't like the way she spoke to him, and he certainly didn't like the way she had prodded him with her toe earlier. Suddenly, the sight of her bending over to retrieve her torch was just too tempting. McGinty lowered his head, pawed the ground – and charged!

Kitty thought that she would burst with the effort of keeping her laughter in, as Margaret squealed, pitched forward and landed face down in the compost heap! It had been a soft landing, but the smell was revolting! Margaret, certain that she had swallowed some of the horrible stuff, felt sick. Giving a groan, she slowly picked herself up, prodding herself gingerly and wrinkling her nose in disgust at the smell. Fighting back angry tears, she hissed, 'You evil little brute!' She began to walk towards McGinty, but he stood his ground and gave Margaret a menacing glare, before lowering his head threateningly again. Margaret stopped in her tracks. Perhaps there was something in this moon madness nonsense after all, and the goat was about to go wild. She certainly didn't want to risk being butted again. Besides, she was cold, tired – and now she needed a bath too! This time she didn't make the mistake of turning her back on McGinty, walking backwards out of the gate and shutting it carefully. Then, limping slightly, she walked away, back towards the school.

Kitty waited for a few minutes before coming out of her hiding place to release McGinty. 'Well done, boy,' she said, bending to hug him. 'You certainly showed *her*! Now, let's get you away from here and back to bed.'

The others, meanwhile, were having a simply marvellous time at their feast, and Amanda was now cutting the big cake that she and Helen had bought.

'Just a small slice for me, please, Amanda,' said Alison, holding her stomach. 'I'm absolutely full!'

'Me too,' said Doris. 'It's been simply super though, hasn't it?'

'I'll say it has,' agreed Janet. 'Though I wish that Kitty would hurry up and come back.'

'Yes, I hope everything has gone according to plan,' Hilary said, looking rather anxious. 'If anything has gone wrong . . .'

'Shh!' Isabel said suddenly, holding up a warning finger. 'I thought I heard a noise in the corridor.'

At once everyone became silent, faces tense and watchful as they listened. There it was – the unmistakable sound of footsteps. But was it Kitty returning? Or was it one of the mistresses? The girls held their breath as the footsteps got closer, stopping right outside the door. Slowly the handle moved, the door creaked open and . . .

'Kitty!' gasped Doris, heaving a sigh of relief. 'Thank heavens!'

Kitty beamed round, her eyes sparkling and cheeks rosy from the cold night air. Then her eyes fell on the plate of food the others had put aside for her and she said, 'Ah, good, I'm starving.'

Flinging her coat aside, she sat down and began to eat hungrily. The others nibbled on their cake and sipped their ginger beer, all of them dying to know what she had been up to.

'Well?' said Janet impatiently, as soon as the girl had cleared her plate. 'How did it go?'

'Very well indeed,' answered Kitty brightly. 'Better

than I could have hoped, in fact. Harriet, do you think that I might have a piece of that chocolate, please?'

Harriet handed the chocolate over and Kitty broke a large chunk off, seeming lost in her own thoughts as she ate it.

'Kitty, we'd quite like to know what happened,' Carlotta prompted her.

'And so you shall, Carlotta, so you shall,' Kitty assured her, before taking a sip of ginger beer.

'Yes, but *when*?' asked Bobby. 'We're simply dying of curiosity.'

'Ah, be patient now, Bobby,' said Kitty. 'Just you wait until tomorrow night.'

'Tomorrow night!' repeated Helen in dismay. 'Kitty, we can't wait that long.'

'Of course we can't,' said Alison. 'Kitty, you must tell us now.'

But Kitty could be as stubborn as McGinty at times. 'Tomorrow,' she said firmly. 'Trust me, it will be well worth the wait.'

'It had better be, you wretch,' said Grace. 'I shan't be able to sleep tonight.'

'Oh yes you will, my girl,' Kitty told her. 'You and I need to go to the darkroom, bright and early!'

McGinty the hero

'I don't think I can face breakfast this morning,' said Alison, with a shudder, as she brushed her hair. 'I ate far too much last night and I feel quite sick now.'

'Serves you right for eating half a packet of chocolate biscuits,' said Bobby, with a grin. 'Gosh, I'm tired. I wish I could go back to bed for an hour instead of going down to breakfast.'

Most of the second and third formers felt either sick or tired, or – in a few cases – both. Only Kitty was her usual bright and breezy self, brushing her hair and getting dressed in record time, and singing all the while.

'Kitty, do you *have* to be so lively – and so noisy – this early in the morning?' groaned Amanda, who was having great difficulty in keeping her eyes open. 'It quite wears me out just to look at you.'

'Ah, but it's a wonderful day,' said the Irish girl, skipping over to look out of the window. 'And I've a feeling it's going to get better. I'm just going to pop next door and see if Grace is up yet.'

'Yes, you go and annoy the second formers,' murmured Doris, who had yet to get out of bed. 'Take your time and don't hurry back.'

'We'll have to try and eat something,' said Hilary, without enthusiasm. 'The mistresses will be most suspicious if we're all off our food.'

'Yes – at the very least we'll be sent to Matron,' said Janet, with a shudder. 'And we all know what that means!'

The others did know. It meant a large dose of extremely nasty-tasting medicine! So the girls made a heroic effort to get through breakfast without arousing suspicion.

'I must say, Kitty,' said Isabel, as she pushed her plate away. 'Whatever happened last night doesn't seem to have had much effect on Margaret. Just look at her.'

At once all eyes turned to the sixth-form table, where Margaret was drinking coffee and chattering to her neighbour as though she hadn't a care in the world.

'Don't all stare at her like that!' hissed Kitty. 'She'll guess that something is up. You see, girls, Margaret doesn't realise yet that she's been caught out. But she'll know all about it before today is over – and you are all going to be there when it dawns on her!'

This sounded good, the third formers exchanging excited glances.

'You know that Mam'zelle's giving a slide show in the hall tonight,' went on Kitty, and a groan went up. Mam'zelle had recently taken a holiday in France, and had been threatening ever since the beginning of term to show everyone her slides. And tonight the whole school had been invited to see them.

'I'd forgotten all about that,' sighed Janet. 'I suppose we'll have to go, though, or old Mam'zelle will be terribly hurt.'

'I'm quite looking forward to it,' said Hilary. 'Mamzelle gets so carried away when she's talking about her beloved France – it might be quite fun.'

'It *will* be fun,' promised Kitty, with a secretive smile. 'Just make sure you're all there.'

And before they could question her further, she slipped from her seat and darted across to the second-form table, to pass the message on to the girls there.

The French mistress walked by just then, and Grace called out to her, 'Mam'zelle! We're so looking forward to your slide show tonight. If you like I could help to lay out the slides for you in the hall beforehand.'

Grace was one of Mam'zelle's favourites, and the mistress beamed down at her, saying, 'Ah, that is indeed kind of you, *ma petite*. Come to the mistresses' common-room after tea and I will give them to you,'

And, patting the second former's head, she went happily on her way, failing to notice the sly wink that Grace directed at Kitty.

It was as the girls were about to leave the dining-room that Miss Theobald entered, looking very stern indeed. 'Girls, please stay where you are,' she called out. 'I am afraid I have some very serious news.'

'Gracious, whatever can have happened?' whispered Isabel.

'I don't know,' answered Pat, with a frown.

146

'Something bad, by the look of things.'

Miss Theobald began to speak. 'I am sorry to have to tell you all that someone has – apparently deliberately – damaged the school's kitchen garden.'

A gasp went round the room, and someone called out, 'Who did it?'

'I would very much like to know the answer to that,' answered Miss Theobald grimly. 'But unfortunately there are no clues.'

Kitty stole a glance at Margaret, smiling to herself at the look of utter bewilderment on the girl's face. She had, of course, expected Miss Theobald to name McGinty as the culprit and couldn't, for the life of her, understand why she hadn't done so. Instead she was saying, 'If anyone knows anything about this dreadful act, I would like them to come and tell me about it, for I am quite determined to track down the person – or people – responsible.'

But how dreadful to think that any of the St Clare's girls would do such a thing! Janet put up her hand and said, 'Miss Theobald, could someone from outside have got in and damaged the garden?'

'It's possible, I suppose, though I can't imagine what motive they would have had,' replied the head. 'Hopefully we will soon find out. That is all I have to say at the moment.'

A babble of voices broke out as the head departed, and it was left to the mistresses to restore order.

Margaret Winters followed Miss Theobald out,

catching up with her outside her study. 'Miss Theobald!' she said. 'Something has just occurred to me.'

'Yes, Margaret?' said the head.

'Well, I don't want to accuse anyone – or anything – unjustly,' said Margaret, at her most earnest. 'But – well, I don't suppose that goat of Kitty Flaherty's could have had anything to do with this, could he? You see, I was reading something the other day, and apparently some animals are affected by the full moon and go quite mad. There was a full moon last night, and perhaps it caused Kitty's goat to run riot in the garden.'

Miss Theobald smiled faintly. 'That was the first thing that occurred to me, too, Margaret. This full-moon madness sounds like a lot of superstitious nonsense to me, but McGinty's healthy appetite and mischievous nature made me suspect him instantly. As soon as the damage was discovered I sent the gardener to check on him. But McGinty was safely in his stall, with the door securely bolted, so it cannot possibly have been him.'

Margaret almost reeled with shock, but managed to hide this from the head, saying lightly, 'Oh well, it was just a thought.'

'And a very good one,' said Miss Theobald. 'I appreciate your concern, Margaret, and if you have any more ideas as to who the culprit could be, please share them with me.'

The head went into her study and Margaret, her mind in a whirl, walked away. She desperately needed to think. It was just possible that McGinty might have managed to jump the fence and make his way back to the stables. But there was no way on earth that he could have locked himself back in! Margaret fretted and puzzled over the mystery, but could not work out how the goat had managed to put himself in the clear like that. The only thing that she was certain of was that her cunning scheme to get both him and his mistress into trouble had failed!

The entire school, girls and mistresses alike, turned up to Mam'zelle's slide show. Hot-tempered the French mistress might be, but she was also big-hearted and everyone was extremely fond of her.

A big screen had been rigged up on the stage and in front of it stood a projector on a table. Grace was there, carefully arranging piles of slides, and she looked up and grinned as the second and third formers filed in. They all knew that she and Kitty had spent a long time in the darkroom that morning, and realised that whatever they had been doing had something to do with the surprise Kitty had planned for Margaret tonight. They took their seats near the front, just behind the chattering first formers. Soon the big hall was filled to bursting and a huge cheer went up when Mam'zelle walked on to the stage and, thoroughly enjoying being the centre of attention, she beamed round for a moment, before holding up her hands for silence.

'Thank you all for coming!' she cried. 'Tonight I take you on a tour of *la belle* France. Miss Adams, if you would be good enough to turn off the lights, we shall begin!'

Miss Adams obliged, and Mam'zelle showed the first slide, which was of the main street of a pretty little French town.

'This is where I grew up,' explained Mam'zelle, a note of pride in her voice. 'And where many of my family still live.'

She went back to the projector and the picture changed. 'Here is the house where I was born. My brother Pierre lives there now, with his wife and their many children.'

And so it went on. The views of France were most interesting, but soon Mam'zelle began to introduce more and more slides of her family, accompanying them with long anecdotes, and some of the girls began to grow a little restless.

'Now I shall show you a picture of my youngest brother,' said Mamzelle proudly. '*Regardez* Alphonse!'

She clicked the slide into place and a shout of laughter went up. '*Tiens*!' cried Mam'zelle, most offended. 'Why do you laugh at the so-handsome Alphonse?'

'It isn't the so-handsome Alphonse, Mam'zelle,' called out a cheeky first former. 'It's the not-so-handsome McGinty!'

Mamzelle spun round so quickly that she almost overbalanced, and saw at once what had made the audience laugh so uproariously. For there on the screen, instead of her brother, was indeed a picture of McGinty. He was in his stall and, bending over him, was a dark figure, its back to the camera.

'*Mon dieu!*' Mamzelle exclaimed. 'How can this be? Never have I taken a photograph of this bad goat!'

Bustling over to the projector she changed the slide – and McGinty appeared again! This time the figure with him was turned towards the camera, and a murmur broke out as everyone recognised the head girl.

'Grrrace!' shouted Mam'zelle angrily. 'You have done this on purpose. It is abominable! The show must be abandoned!'

But Miss Theobald chanced to look round at Margaret. The girl was huddled in her seat, red-faced, looking as if she wanted the ground to open up and swallow her. 'No, Mam'zelle,' said the head, standing up. 'I would like you to carry on. Please show the next slide.'

The second and third formers caught one another's eyes, alight with excitement. Clever little Kitty! Margaret had stirred up trouble for their forms by using her camera – and now Kitty had turned the tables on her! Several slides followed, each more shocking than the last. There was Margaret, entering the kitchen garden, pulling McGinty behind her. Then shocked gasps and angry murmurs ran round the hall as the head girl was caught in the act of ripping a plant from the ground, an expression of real spite on her face as she did so.

At the back of the hall, Jenny Mills and Barbara Thompson exchanged shocked glances. Neither of them particularly liked Margaret, but they would never have believed that she was capable of such meanness. But the mood in the hall changed completely when the final picture appeared on the screen. Kitty had caught the moment perfectly, and the school was treated to the sight of Margaret sprawling in a most undignified manner on the compost heap, while McGinty stood triumphantly nearby. A great cheer arose, and a group of excitable first formers cried, 'Hurrah for McGinty!' Then the screen went blank, and Miss Adams turned the lights back on.

The French mistress, still a little dazed and bewildered by the turn of events, blinked, while Miss Theobald said, 'A most interesting and informative evening, Mam'zelle. Margaret, I will deal with you tomorrow.'

With that the head left, in her usual calm, dignified manner. Margaret, meanwhile, felt far from calm and dignified as she got to her feet and faced the hard, scornful eyes of her fellow pupils. Even the mistresses looked at her with utter contempt. It was more than she could bear and, with a sob, she fled from the hall.

'Something got your goat, Margaret?' Doris called after her, and everyone roared with laughter.

'Phew!' said Pat. 'That was quite a show!'

'Wasn't it just!' exclaimed Janet. 'And to think I was worried that it was going to be boring.'

Isabel looked across at Kitty, who was being clapped on the back by a group of fourth formers, and laughed. 'Nothing is ever boring when Kitty Flaherty is around!'

18

Margaret in disgrace

Kitty was the heroine of the hour. Word had soon spread that she was responsible for Margaret's disgrace and, as the girls gathered in the dining-room for cocoa and biscuits before bedtime, many of them came up to congratulate her.

'It's about time that someone showed Margaret up for the sly creature that she is. Well done, Kitty!'

'How I wish I could have been there when McGinty butted her into the compost heap. Priceless, Kitty!'

'Thanks to you we won't have to put up with her as head girl any longer, Kitty. Good work!'

'My goodness,' murmured Hilary to the twins. 'Much more of this and Kitty's head will be so big that she won't be able to get through the door.'

But Kitty, as usual, seemed quite unaffected by the praise heaped upon her, saying modestly, 'Ah, it was nothing, to be sure. I couldn't have done it without Grace, for she lent me her camera and taught me how to use it, as well as doing all the hard work in the darkroom.'

So Grace received three cheers as well, then the mistresses decided that there had been quite enough excitement for one evening and ushered the lower forms off to bed.

'Do you suppose Margaret will be expelled?' asked Alison, as she changed into her pyjamas.

'It will serve her right if she is,' said Mirabel. 'I've seen some rotten tricks but, my word, that one takes the biscuit!'

'Yes, to destroy the garden was downright wicked – and then to try and blame it on poor McGinty. Horrible!' said Gladys, wrinkling her nose in distaste.

'Well "poor" McGinty certainly stuck up for himself all right,' said Bobby, with a grin.

'He did that,' agreed Kitty. 'Sure and I was proud of him!'

'Come on, everybody – into bed!' called Janet. 'Lights out in a minute.'

There was some grumbling, but everyone obeyed, secretly quite glad to settle down after all the fun and games. What an evening it had been!

Margaret did not appear at breakfast the next morning and no one was very surprised.

'I wouldn't want to face the whole school if I had behaved as she has,' said Hilary. 'Just imagine how humiliated she must feel.'

Margaret did indeed feel most humiliated – and frightened as well. She had barely slept at all that night, trying to think of some way to explain her extraordinary behaviour to Miss Theobald. At last she had realised that it was pointless to try and talk her way out of it. She would just have to accept whatever punishment the head decided to give her. And it was certain to be a big punishment! And all because of that wretched Kitty Flaherty. Margaret could not see that she had brought everything on herself, thanks to her own spite. For that would have meant admitting to a fault – something Margaret would never do. This was the end of her brief career as head girl, she knew. Never again would Miss Theobald trust her. She might even be expelled. That thought caused a chill to run down Margaret's spine. The disgrace would be simply unbearable, and her parents would be so angry, and so bitterly disappointed in her. She was not looking forward to her interview with Miss Theobald at all.

But before the head dealt with Margaret, she sent for Kitty.

'Good morning, Mam,' the Irish girl greeted Miss Theobald politely as she entered the study.

'Good morning, Kitty,' replied the Head. 'Please sit down.'

Kitty did so, and Miss Theobald looked at her thoughtfully for a moment, before saying, 'I am going to ask you something, Kitty, and I would like a truthful answer. Were those slides last night your work?'

'Indeed they were, Mam,' answered Kitty at once, looking the headmistress straight in the eye. 'And, as you'll have guessed, I wasn't in my bed when I should have been. I know I'll probably be punished for that but, you see, I knew Margaret was going to try and have

McGinty sent away and I had to save him. What's more, Mam, I wanted you and everyone else to know what kind of person Margaret is. Sure and I'm awful sorry about the garden, and if I'd known she meant to damage it like that then perhaps I would have come up with another plan, but there, she started pulling the plants up, and throwing them around, and there was no stopping her!'

And there was no stopping Kitty when she had a tale to tell, thought Miss Theobald, amused despite the seriousness of the situation. Now that the girl had paused to take a breath, the head opened her mouth. But before she could utter a word, Kitty was off again. 'And there's something else you should know, Mam. Margaret was the one who caused all that trouble for Jenny Mills and the second form. Though, of course, the second formers didn't get punished in the end, for we third formers owned up and –'

'Kitty!'

'Yes, Mam?' said Kitty, looking a little surprised at the interruption.

'Do stop for a moment, my dear, for my head is quite in a whirl!' said Miss Theobald. 'Now, please explain everything to me calmly and clearly.'

Kitty did her best, though Miss Theobald had to interrupt once or twice when she got carried away! But, at last, the head knew the whole story. 'Well!' she said at last, sitting back in her chair and looking quite astonished. 'It seems that Margaret has been behind quite a lot of the unpleasantness that has occurred at St Clare's this term.'

Kitty nodded, then said impulsively, 'Mam, will you make Jenny head girl again now?'

'I would like to very much, Kitty,' answered the head, looking thoughtful. 'But I must bear in mind that she, too, did wrong.'

'Yes,' said Kitty. 'But what Jenny did was a – a good wrong!'

'A good wrong?' repeated Miss Theobald, puzzled.

'Well, you see, although Jenny broke the rules, she did it with good intentions,' explained Kitty. 'She only wanted to protect the second formers and keep them out of trouble. Whereas everything Margaret did . . .'

'Was intended to deliberately cause trouble for others,' the head finished for her.

'Exactly!' Kitty leaned forward and said confidingly, 'You know, Mam, I think that here at St Clare's we need a head girl that everyone likes, and trusts, and can look up to. And, in Jenny, that's exactly what we had.'

'I can see that you have given the matter a lot of thought, Kitty,' said Miss Theobald, smiling, but thinking privately that there was a great deal of wisdom and truth in the girl's words. 'And I shall give it some thought too. I shall let the heads of form know what I decide.'

Kitty stood up, but before she left the room, she said, 'Am I to be punished, for being out in the grounds the other night, Mam?'

Miss Theobald looked hard at the girl for a moment. At last she said, 'No, Kitty. For what you did was also a "good wrong", as you like to call it. Without your intervention I would probably never have seen Margaret's true character.'

Exactly what passed between the head and Margaret, no one ever found out. But one of the fourth formers reported seeing the girl come out of Miss Theobald's room in tears later that morning. That afternoon her parents were sent for, prompting rumours that Margaret had been expelled. But, after a long talk with Miss Theobald, Mr and Mrs Winters left alone, both of them pale and grim-faced.

'As Margaret only has one more term left at St Clare's, she is being allowed to stay,' announced Janet in the common-room that evening. She and Grace, along with the other form heads, had been summoned to Miss Theobald's study earlier, and had just returned with the news. 'I rather think she has her parents to thank for that. They are going to pay for the damage to the garden, and Mr Winters has promised to try and talk some sense into her during the holidays.'

'Well, let's hope he succeeds,' said Hilary. 'Perhaps Margaret can learn something from this and become a nicer person as a result.'

'I saw her outside earlier,' said Alison. 'She looked awfully pale, and so red-eyed that I almost felt sorry for her.'

'Alison!' shouted everyone, exasperated.

'I said *almost*,' huffed Alison. 'Then I remembered how she betrayed my trust, and caused trouble over our trick, and how she tried to get McGinty sent away. So I don't feel sorry for her at all any more.'

'Thank heavens for that!' said Pat. 'Janet, did Miss Theobald say anything about who is to be head girl now?'

'Yes, I was just coming to that,' said Janet, smiling broadly. 'Jenny Mills is to be head girl for the rest of this term *and* next term. And Barbara Thompson is going to be her deputy.'

'That's marvellous!' cried Doris. 'It will be wonderful to have Jenny back again, and Barbara's a good sort too.'

Everyone agreed heartily with this, and both forms felt highly honoured when, just before bedtime, the head girl herself dropped into the common-room.

'I just wanted to thank you all,' said Jenny, smiling round. 'I know it's because of you kids that I'm head girl again, and I can't tell you how thrilled I am. Kitty, you deserve a medal!'

Kitty laughed and said, 'Sure, Jenny, and it's McGinty you ought to be thanking. He's the real hero.'

'Yes, I've alredy been to see McGinty, and taken him some biscuits as a treat,' said Jenny. 'Judging by the way he snatched them from my hand I think he enjoyed them!'

'Well, wasn't that nice of her?' said Amanda, once Jenny had left. 'You know, now that everything has turned out right, I think I'm going to enjoy the rest of the term.'

'What's left of it,' said Carlotta. 'Only one week to go and then it's home for the hols.'

Kitty sighed. 'It's home for good as far as McGinty and I are concerned.'

'Golly, so it is!' cried Isabel. 'I'd forgotten you were only with us for one term, Kitty. You've fitted in so well it feels as if you've been here forever.'

'We shall miss you both,' said Bobby, looking glum. 'I don't suppose your people will decide to stay in London a bit longer, so that you can spend next term with us too?'

Kitty shook her head. 'I'm afraid not. Father's finished his research, so they're coming to collect me on the last day of term, then it's back to Kilblarney for all of us. I'm looking forward to going home and seeing my old friends, of course, but McGinty and I will really hate saying goodbye to St Clare's.'

'Everything's changing,' sighed Grace. 'Tomorrow night we second formers are moving into our new common-room.'

'Ooh yes!' said Doris brightly. 'Well, that's good news, anyway. It'll be nice to come in here and be able to bag a seat without you great, lazy lumps hogging all the comfy chairs. Ow! No, Grace, don't! I was only joking!'

Everyone laughed as Grace began pummelling Doris with a cushion, and the atmosphere in the room brightened again.

Home for the holidays

'Peace, perfect peace!' sighed Hilary happily, putting her feet up on a sofa and stretching out.

'Yes, isn't it grand,' said Pat, gazing round the common-room, which seemed very much bigger now that it was only occupied by one form. 'Although I must admit, I got to like most of the second formers very much in the end.'

'Me too,' agreed Janet. 'Who would have thought that we'd actually grow quite fond of the little beasts?'

'I say, has anyone seen Amanda?' asked Isabel. 'She promised to lend me a book to read, but I haven't seen her in simply ages.'

'She's probably in the second form's common-room,' said Carlotta. 'I saw her arm-in-arm with Helen a little while ago. Those two are almost inseparable these days.'

'Oh well, I'll just have to come and chat to you, Pat,' said Isabel cheerfully, going to sit by her twin.

'You know, Isabel, it's only natural that Amanda should want to spend more time with the second form, and get to know them better, as she's going to be joining them next term,' said Pat, watching her twin closely. 'And it's a very good thing that she and

161

Helen have become such good friends.'

'Absolutely,' agreed Isabel at once. 'The news about the baby has worked wonders on both of them.'

'Well, I must say, you're taking it awfully well,' said Pat.

Isabel looked puzzled for a moment, then her brow cleared and she laughed. 'Pat, I like Amanda enormously, and I'm pleased to have her as a friend. But I don't mind at all that she's spending more time with the second form.'

'Really?' said Pat.

'Really,' said Isabel. 'I think you and I have both learned a valuable lesson this term. That no matter how many friends we make, no one will ever come between us.'

Pat nodded solemnly. 'You're quite right, old thing. I say, won't it be fun next term to come back to school together, and to have our beds next to one another again.'

'I'll say,' agreed Isabel. 'But let's not talk about next term just yet. We have the holidays to enjoy first, and I'm looking forward to them so much.'

All of the girls were looking forward to the holidays, and the last few days of term simply flew by. Then – all of a sudden, it seemed – it was the last day of term and everyone was packing to go home.

In the third form's dormitory there was complete chaos, and girls hunted high and low for missing stockings, lost toothbrushes, and a dozen other things that seemed, unaccountably, to have disappeared.

Hilary, who was always very well organised, and had packed most of her things the night before, was looking out of the window. Suddenly she cried, 'Good gracious, someone's parents have arrived early. Why, Kitty, I do believe they're yours!'

'No, mine wouldn't turn up at this hour, Hilary. They know that it always takes me ages to pack.'

Carlotta, who had joined Hilary by the window, looked out and said, 'They *are* yours, Kitty. I recognise your father's red hair.'

'Now, what do you suppose they're playing at?' said Kitty, sounding mildly annoyed. 'Ah well, I suppose I'd better go down and greet them.'

The rest of the third form, glad of an excuse to abandon the task of packing for a while, followed the Irish girl downstairs, where they found Mr and Mrs Flaherty in the big entrance hall. They looked rather lost, but their faces lit up when Kitty appeared, and she ran towards them, hugging first one, then the other.

'But, Mother, what are you doing here so early?' asked the Irish girl at last.

'Why, you asked us to collect you soon after breakfast, dear,' said Mrs Flaherty.

'No, I didn't,' said Kitty, puzzled.

'Ah now, you did,' said her mother, reaching into her handbag. 'Sure and here's a letter from you that came a few days ago. See, it says "Looking forward to seeing you soon after breakfast".'

Kitty took the sheet of paper, frowning over it for a

moment. Then she gave a laugh and said, 'It says "Looking forward to seeing you soon". Then there's a full stop and a new sentence, which begins "After breakfast" – and then I went on to tell you about something I was doing that day. Honestly, Mother!'

The watching third formers laughed as Mr Flaherty peered over Kitty's shoulder and said, 'Sure and it is a full stop. I can see it now. Ah well, we're here now, so what's to be done?'

At that moment Matron came bustling into the hall, crying, 'You third formers should be upstairs packing!' Then she spotted Kitty's parents.

'Hallo there. Have you come to collect one of the girls?'

'We have indeed, Mam,' said Mr Flaherty. 'But it seems we're a little early.'

'My goodness, there's no need to ask whose parents you are,' said Matron, her plump face creasing into a smile. 'Now you come along with me, Mr and Mrs Flaherty, and we'll see if we can find you a cup of tea. And you girls, go and finish your packing – unless you want to spend the holidays at school!'

Much as they loved St Clare's, no one did wish to spend the holidays there, and the girls sped away.

Seeing her parents seemed to have spurred Kitty on, for she finished her packing in record time, then dashed out of the room.

'I say, where's Kitty gone in such a hurry?' asked Bobby. 'I hope she hasn't left without saying goodbye.'

'No, for she's left her case here,' said Gladys. 'I

daresay she'll be back shortly.'

Kitty was back shortly, but she wasn't alone – for she was accompanied by McGinty, looking very jaunty at the prospect of new surroundings. The girls greeted him warmly and Janet laughed, 'If Matron comes in and sees him she'll blow her top!'

'No, boy, you can't come home with me,' said Mirabel, as the little goat tried to scramble into her case. 'And I hope your hooves aren't muddy, for you've just trodden all over my pyjamas!'

'Now behave yourself, McGinty,' said Kitty sternly, pulling him away. 'Oh dear, perhaps bringing him in here wasn't such a good idea.'

'Well, we'll have to leave in a minute, so he won't have time to get into much mischief,' said Pat, shutting her case. 'Are you ready, Isabel? The coach will be here soon.'

Downstairs was a hive of activity as girls ran around saying goodbye to mistresses, exchanging addresses and making arrangements to meet in the holidays, all at the tops of their voices.

Matron appeared and clapped her hands over her ears, crying, 'My goodness, I've never heard such a dreadful racket! I thought there was a riot going on in here.' Then she caught sight of McGinty and shouted, 'Kitty Flaherty! What is that goat doing here?'

Mr Flaherty, who – along with his wife – had followed Matron into the hall, said, 'Don't you worry, Mam. We'll take Kitty and McGinty off your hands now.

And I daresay you'll be glad to see the back of them, for they're troublesome creatures, the both of them!'

'Well, I don't know about that,' said Matron, her face softening. 'They've certainly brightened things up around here.'

'Have I given everyone my address?' asked Kitty, picking up her case. 'Now, don't forget, everyone, if you're ever in Kilblarney be sure to drop in.'

'Kee-ty!' came a voice from behind her, and the girl turned to see Mam'zelle coming towards her, arms outstretched. 'So, the time has come for you to leave us,' she said, giving the astonished Kitty a big hug and planting a smacking kiss on each of her cheeks. 'Ah, what trouble you have caused us this term, you and that bad goat. But we shall miss you.'

Then, to Kitty's further amazement, the French mistress bent down and tickled the little goat under his whiskery chin. This was exactly where he liked to be tickled most, and McGinty decided that Mam'zelle, who had never been a great favourite of his, wasn't such a bad sort after all. A bowl of freshly cut flowers stood on a low table nearby and, turning his head, the goat plucked one out. Holding it between his teeth, he gently nudged Mam'zelle, the watching girls helpless with laughter as she took it from him and tucked it behind her ear. The spectacle was so comical that even Miss Jenks and Miss Adams couldn't hide their smiles, as a delighted Mam'zelle cried, 'See! He is not a bad goat after all, but a good one!'

'Sure and he is that, Mam,' said Doris, imitating Kitty's accent to perfection and making everyone laugh even louder.

'Goodbye, Kitty – don't forget to write! Goodbye, McGinty!'

And, amid a chorus of farewells and a sea of waving handkerchiefs, Kitty, her parents and McGinty left.

Hilary sighed. 'Blow! I do wish Kitty could have stayed on. She was such fun.'

'Cheer up, Hilary,' said Isabel, patting her on the shoulder. 'I know it's not going to be quite the same without her, but I daresay there will be more new girls to meet next term.'

'Pat! Isabel!' said Amanda. 'You will write to me in the hols, won't you?'

'Of course we will,' Isabel assured her. 'Well, I certainly will – and Pat will, as long as she doesn't go falling out of any more trees and breaking her arm again!'

'No fear of that,' said Pat. 'I'm going to sit quietly and not move from the sofa at all during the holidays, so I shall be perfectly safe.'

'Come on, Amanda!' called Helen, rushing up to the third formers. 'Mummy and Daddy are here.'

'Marvellous!' said Amanda, smiling widely. 'I can't wait to see them both. Wonder if they've thought of any names for the baby yet.'

And, arm-in-arm, chattering happily, the two stepsisters walked off.

'Well, if you'd told me at the beginning of term that

those two would end up being the best of friends, I would never have believed it,' said Bobby.

'It's been a strange term altogether,' said Pat. 'Who could have guessed that Jenny would resign as head girl? Or that Margaret would get up to such mean, underhand tricks?'

'Or that you and Isabel would fall out,' put in Carlotta.

'Thank goodness everything turned out all right in the end,' said Isabel. 'And Pat and I are never going to quarrel again!'

'Come along, train girls!' came Matron's booming voice. 'The coach has arrived to take you to the station.'

And, with a flurry of last-minute goodbyes, the girls left St Clare's to go home for the holidays.

'Let's hope that we don't have as much trouble as we have had this term when we come back,' said Isabel, as the coach moved away. 'I could do with a nice, peaceful term.'

'I don't expect you'll get one,' laughed Pat. 'I don't know why, but there *always* seems to be something happening at St Clare's!'